The Accidental Animal Cop

The Brownville Series

Stevie Lynne

Stanhy Publications

It takes a village, especially when you are writing about one! My thanks to the many people in my life who encourage me, keep me grounded and most importantly, those who give me inspiration for writing these stories! You know who you are...

Dedication

To all of the men and women who devote their lives to caring for all things great and small.

Chapter One

R oger broke up with me the night I burned the K of C Hall down.

It wasn't like I MEANT to burn it down; sometimes these things just kinda happen.

You see, there was a family of squirrels that were in the attic, had been all spring. Caleb Moss, the fat old man who took care of the hall, was always calling me to come get them out. Of course, no matter how many times I removed one red squirrel from residence, three more were sneaking back in behind me.

By the fourth time he called, I decided it was time to remove them permanently.

"Are you sure you know what you're doing?" Caleb had yelled up at me for like probably the twentieth time while I perched on the shaky ladder balanced on the second floor roof. The eave window of the attic was just within reach, the last access to the entire third story. I had already crawled around inside on my hands and knees as hundred-year-old wood slivers stabbed my knees and hands. I sighed as I struggled to keep the ladder balanced and still maneuver the gopher bomb in my right hand.

"Relax, Caleb. It'll be over in a few seconds."

"The package says you shouldn't use it in a building!"

"It'll be fine, Caleb. Trust me."

I lit the fuse and tossed it in the attic window; the ladder swaying as I tossed it.

And the interior lit up with a whoosh.

Squirrels launched through the window in a chattering frenzy, nails scrabbling across the wooden shingled exterior. One bounced off my chest as the ladder started tipping, leaning impossibly far to the right. I yelped as my fingers closed around the old gingerbread molding that lined the front eave of the building. The ladder fell free of my legs as squirrels used me as a launching pad. Dimly, I heard Caleb's shouts as smoke billowed into my face, tearing my eyes and filling my lungs.

I landed in the forsythia bushes, with a really pissed off red squirrel's front teeth sunk into the ball of my thumb.

Morosely I watched as the 109-year-old hall smoked and sparked. The Brownville Fire Department sprayed jets of water into the eaves, turning black smoke into steam. My phone chimed with an incoming text. I tugged it out of my pocket and looked at the name.

Roger.

My heart gave a little flip-flop like it always did when I saw his name, even three and a half years later. Then I read the message, and it dropped like a stone.

A burning ember floated down and landed on my hand. I yelped, flinging the phone into the street, where it exploded in a starburst of glass and plastic. Firefighter Cowen looked at me wide eyed.

"Rachel, are you okay?"

"I'm fine, just FINE!"

And I burst into tears.

Sometimes, I wish I had just learned how to make a damned cappuccino properly.

Chapter Two

It was my lack of skill at the espresso machine that landed me on the lawn of the K of C hall four months later. I had graduated from the University of Vermont in May, my shiny new Computer Science degree in my hot little hand...and promptly couldn't find a job.

In a way, that was kind of okay. Because to be honest, I was having some doubt about whether I wanted to sit around and stare at a screen all day, anyway. I hadn't switched majors, mostly because Roger was in most of my classes.

And Roger was the reason why I found myself behind the counter at Java Joe's, struggling to make sense of cappuccinos and lattes.

"You didn't just put the foam in first, did you?" The pink-haired girl across from me had a barbell in her eyebrow. Steam shot out of the wand, spraying at me as I tilted the pitcher the wrong way yet again. My face was beginning to look like I had a chemical peel.

"Yeah, I did. Why?"

"Because that is not how you make a cappuccino! That's a latte!"

"So what? It's all the same."

"No, it ISN'T! It's not the same at ALL!"

I sighed, slamming down the pitcher. "Honey, you ordered a single shot, decaf cappuccino with skim milk and Splenda...that isn't the same either! Christ, do you shower with your socks on too?"

My first job out of school lasted all of four hours.

Roger was home when I came in, reeking of coffee, my one and only paycheck in my back pocket, sputtering about the nerve of these ingrate college kids.

"What happened to your face?"

"Steam from the espresso machine. I got fired today."

"Huh." He went back to reading some paperwork. "Oh, your Uncle Jim called. Wants you to call him back as soon as you can."

"Did you even hear me? I got fired."

"Yeah, I heard." He didn't look up.

Exasperated, I stomped into the kitchen and called Uncle Jim back. He was my favorite uncle, the cool one. He was also a lieutenant for the police in my hometown, a job that had always fascinated me. Uncle Jim was probably the only relative I could handle talking to right then.

Twenty minutes later, I hit the end button on my phone, frowning as I considered what he had just told me. Roger came into the kitchen, popping open the refrigerator door and staring morosely at the contents.

"Are you going shopping soon?"

"Yeah, well, when I cash my check, I guess."

"What did your uncle want?"

I laughed, a bit disbelievingly. "He called to offer me a job."

Roger finally looked at me. "Really? What kind of job?"

"As the Animal Control Officer for Brownville."

"As the...what?"

"You heard me. He asked me if I would be the Animal Control Officer for Brownville, at least until they can find a permanent person. I told him no."

"Now whoa there, hold on. You told him no?"

"Roger, it would mean moving back to Brownville. I couldn't live here and work there." That was a good fifty miles away from the college town we currently lived in.

Roger leaned against the refrigerator for a moment in silence. "Well, um. I think maybe you should reconsider this."

"Reconsider this? Why? I don't want to have an hour commute every day."

"Um. Well, Rach, I guess this is as good a time to tell you as any. I've been offered an internship."

"You have? Where? Oh my God, that's great!" Roger was a brilliant programmer.

He looked down at the ground and didn't answer. The first prickle of unease wormed its way into my brain.

"Where is it, Roger?"

"Cambridge."

"Cambridge?" Well, that would be different, but okay. Cambridge was a vital area, jobs were plentiful. I had a girlfriend who had moved to Boston, someone who could help us get on our feet socially. "Cambridge will be a good gig! We'll be closer to the city, to all kinds of jobs for you and me. When does this start?"

"It's in Cambridge, England."

"What?" England? Like Great Britain? Holy cow!

He finally looked me in the eye. "It's for a year. They're

going to give me housing and relocate me. I was going to talk to you about it before now, but..."

"Me? They're giving me housing? What about WE?"

"There's only housing for single men. Look, it's only a year. We won't change, I know it will be different, but...we can Skype, maybe you can even come visit while I'm there. It's a huge opportunity for me. So why don't you take this job in Brownville? You can move home and..."

"What did you tell them?"

He hung his head. "It's just for a year."

"Roger? What did you tell them?"

He looked me in the eye. "Yes. I said yes. I'm leaving in two weeks."

Chapter Three

"The Captain's been getting calls all day about the K of C Hall."

I groaned, "I know, I know. How was I to know you couldn't use a gopher bomb inside a building?"

Uncle Jim raised one eyebrow at me. "Rachel, it said so right on the package."

"God, I know, I know, everyone's been telling me, okay? Look, it wasn't a really big fire, and they needed renovating anyway, so.."

"Jesus! Rachel Ann Tillison! Don't you dare say that again!" He rubbed his hands over his face. I sighed.

He also heaved a sigh, then pushed a piece of paper at me. "Here. We got a loose dog complaint over on Sycamore Street. Do you think you can go get it without causing major damage to anything?"

I snuffled, rubbing the back of my hand across my nose. My eyes still burned from smoke and tears. I hadn't really processed Roger's defection yet, despite a marathon Skype session with him last night.

Uncle Jim eyed me suspiciously. "What's wrong?"

"Nothing's wrong."

"Rachel, I've known you for 22 years now and I know when something's wrong, so what is it?"

"Jim, why don't you let her be?" the voice came from the hall behind me. Sandy Case, Uncle Jim's girlfriend, came into the room. His eyes went past me to her, a flush starting up his cheeks. Uncle Jim didn't have a very good poker face.

"Hey Sandy. Thanks. Look, I gotta go. Things to do and all." I picked up the paper and headed out the door. She patted my shoulder as I passed her. "Hang in there, Rachel." I felt a prickling in my eyes at the kindness in her voice.

I stomped down the stairs of the Brownville Police Department and headed towards the Paddy Waggin'. That was the cutesie name bestowed on an aging, battered Chevy minivan in a soft puke green. I yanked the driver's door open, wincing at the metal on metal screech it made, the puff of wet dog smell released from the interior. This wasn't exactly what I envisioned last May when I threw my tasseled cap in the air with the other graduates of my class. Dropping into the saggy seat, I allowed myself a few minutes to wallow in self-pity.

Was it my breasts? I looked down at my sadly shapeless chest, my 32Bs hidden under the poly blend uniform shirt I wore. He had always made remarks about liking big boobs. Maybe it was my face, with my too wide eyes and too narrow nose and my skin still prone to breaking out. I eyed myself in the rear-view mirror for a moment, convinced a massive breakout must be lurking.

No. No acne burbling to the surface. I didn't look any different. I felt it but I was still the same, flat chested, too narrow nose and unruly, short brown hair. I had the same eyes as my Mom and Uncle Jim did, bright blue, maybe my only real noticeable feature that I had. Otherwise, I was just average Rachel, the girl whose ex-boyfriend was dining on the Thames River with his new love, Courtney, while I schlepped off to find some dog. Rachel the high school basketball player, Rachel the girl whose family owned a farm. Not a Courtney, whose dad owned an airline (but a small one, just a charter service, Roger had told me) and was attending graduate school in London. I was just Rachel, the new dog officer, er, excuse me, Animal Control Officer, of Brownville, VT.

Whoop de do.

The radio scratched into life.

"Brown ACO, this is dispatch, copy?" Uncle Jim's voice.

"Brown ACO by."

"Brown ACO, we received a call that the dog from the earlier complaint was just spotted over on Meadow Lane, near the tracks. Jan Bower says it won't let her grab him, but it's still in the area. Said it's at, uh..140 Meadow Lane."

"Roger that, dispatch, Brown ACO out."

Screw Roger. Time to go catch myself a dog.

Chapter Four

I used the shortcut over the train tracks to get to the Meadows. Uncle Jim would stroke out if he knew, but it took minutes off the time it took to get over there. Last year, Sandy got hung up on the tracks and destroyed her car, making everyone kinda antsy about the crossing. Then she led a couple of Russian mobsters across it and got them hung up on purpose. They both died, squished under the 3:30 Maine to Georgia. After that, the town started making noise about either closing it or forcing the railroad to put gates up there.

I was glad today they hadn't done anything about it yet.

You had to know how to do it. You had to angle the car just so to catch the two high spots on the rails, so the entire car cleared and didn't get stuck. You also had to not be a dummy and do it when the trains were coming. The next one wasn't due for two hours yet, so I wasn't too worried about that.

The crossing was a weird bump in the road, kind of like they decided last minute to put one there. It raised you up a dozen feet or more above the road; the tracks cutting a swath through dense forest, tall dank pines crowding maples with changing leaves. I was busy watching my path over the tracks when motion caught my eye.

Something white...and huge...flitted through the trees at the edge of the tracks, some thirty feet down from where I was. I stopped.

What the heck was that?

I grew up around these woods, spent my entire life until four years ago here, and I hadn't ever seen anything big and white in the woods. I peered through the window. Another flash of white, further away now, a big area, several feet off the ground, a ripple of movement.

Was it a cow? I caught another glimpse, movement like something walking, then gone, the only notice of its having been there were leaves still nodding on the tree along the tracks.

Huh. I made a mental note to stop by the Addisons' place after work and let them know one of their heifers might be loose.

I pulled up alongside Jan Bower's house a couple minutes later and spied her over-sized hat bobbing in her garden. It looked like she was harvesting cut flowers, probably for the farmer's market at the high school tomorrow. She heard the wheezing exhaust of the Paddy Waggin' as I pulled up.

"Afternoon, Mrs. Bower."

"Rachel. How are you?" She laid down the bundle of flowers and let herself through the garden gate. She was old, like late sixties, really nice lady, all apple cheeks and kind eyes.

"I'm good. Uncle Jim said you had a stray dog out here?"

"Yes, I thought he was going to let me come up to him,

but he bolted. Say, what happened out at the K of C hall yesterday?"

I groaned. "Oh, er, uh...."

Her eyes twinkled. "Never mind. Forget I asked."

I felt my cheeks burn. "So, um. Where exactly did you see this dog?"

She turned away from me to look back down the road. "I saw him a couple times today, a big Shepherd looking dog, a grey and brown one. He was around the backyard this morning, looked right at me and skeedaddled. Then I saw him again, an hour or so later. This time he wasn't quite so quick to run, acted like he wanted to come to me. Then, just now, I saw him down there, at the edge of the field over there." She pointed to a raggedy milk weed filled field that edged the road just south of us.

"Any tags or collar?"

She shook her head no, the hat brim vibrating with the motion. "No, nothing I could see. Seemed scared, like he wanted to be back with people." She tended to see the good in everything and everyone.

"Alright. I'll go look around. Thanks Mrs. Bower."

"Good luck with him, honey."

I backed out onto Meadow Lane and headed south. The earliest leaves were starting to turn, patches of red and gold in the forest. I pulled off and parked alongside the field, rummaged around for my dog catching tools. A can of dog treats, and a long pole with a loop, known as a rabies pole, a slip lead in my back pocket. I looked around the empty lot, not seeing anything dog like. Still, you had to try.

"Hey puppy! Come here, come'ere boy!" I put two fingers in my mouth and produced a piercing whistle, a Tillison family specialty.

The silence hung undisturbed. Late season butterflies

floated between the milkweed plants in drifts of orange and black. No dog. Sighing, I drew a deep breath and placed my fingers in my mouth again, ready to blow apart the stillness with one last whistle.

The sound died in my throat in a gargle as the leaves rustled fiercely...some 6 feet off the ground. I froze, my fingers still jammed in my mouth as my heart rate ratcheted up. A patch of white appeared, with one large, liquid brown eye, peering between two dying branches of maple leaves. We regarded each other for a long moment, then the eye sank back into the darkness and was gone. It left quivering leaves and the sound of something heavy moving away from me...fast.

"What the hell was that?" My voice sounded squeaky to my ears. I finally reacted, running towards the woods where I had seen it. Dank, musty leaf smells assailed my nose as I carefully parted the branches, looking up over my head at where the eye had been. Holy moly! It was probably closer to seven feet off the ground instead of six! What the heck was this?

The ground underfoot was churned up, torn up by something large that had sunk into the soft dirt. I spied a track, large cloven hoof separate from the rest, clear as a bell.

"Man! That's gotta be an ox or something. No heifer I know is that big." My voice was loud in the still air, spooking me. Suddenly, I no longer wanted to be in the woods anymore, no matter how visible the tracks were leading away from me. And visible they were, a dark churned up path leading straight back from where I stood.

I backed out of the woods slowly, my heart knocking in my chest. Screw it. If the dog wasn't here, I was heading back to town.

Chapter Five

My radio was going off when I reached the Paddy Waggin' again. Groaning silently, I keyed the mic.

"This is Brown ACO, over."

"Brown ACO, are you still over in the Meadows?" Uncle Jim again.

"Roger that. No sign of that dog. Hey, would you call Addison's and ask them if they are missing a steer out this way? I just saw something huge and white in the woods. Gotta be a steer or something."

"Okay. Will do. Listen Rach, I have another call for you out that way, down over to Dunbarton Lane. Mrs. Homas is complaining that Bobby Beleeno's birds are in her yard again. I can't raise him by phone, and she's about losing her mind over it. Can you go catch them up?"

"What am I supposed to do with 'em once I get 'em?" I didn't know I had to collect birds too. "And what kind of birds are these?"

"She didn't say. She was pretty upset. Hang on...let me pull up the last inspection report Joe did."

Joe Dummers was the former ACO and animal inspector in town, by all accounts a crotchety old man who had simply walked in and retired abruptly one day. As the animal inspector, he would have been in charge of going around to all the homes with animals and counting them. This was a resource for us when we had to deal with going in to these places on any kind of complaint. As I waited for Uncle Jim to get back to me with what Bobby had, I wondered if they were going to send me out for the inspections now. Uncle Jim's voice scratched over the radio again.

"Brown ACO, it says here, uh, 42 chickens, seven ducks, a half dozen turkeys and three 'other'."

"Other? What the heck is that supposed to mean?"

"I don't know, maybe peacocks or something? It's probably his chickens in Mrs. Homas's yard. They get out all the time."

"What do I do with them, then?"

"Just bring them back over to his place after. We'll call him and warn him about making sure his birds don't get out anymore."

"Alright. Brown ACO en route."

I gave a last look around the deserted field as I turned the key in the ignition. Butterflies still drifted through the sunbaked grass. No dog. My eyes went to the spot where I had seen the enormous eye. Nothing. A chill snaked up my back.

I backed the van out of the field and headed over to Mrs. Homas.

Chapter Six

The Homas's had a cute little one-story stone house that kind of rambled alongside the lane for a way. The front was embellished with lavish gardens. White trimmed doors and windows peeked out of fieldstone walls. A large oak tree shaded one corner of it, a neatly kept split-rail fence protecting the front and curving around towards the rear of the property.

Mrs. Homas was a short, roly-poly woman prone to bad perms. She was waiting for me when I arrived. And she was almost hysterical.

"You have to get it! Get it out of my yard! Now! I can't believe that thing is over here! He shouldn't have that. Why won't you people make him get rid of it?"

She clutched her little fluffy white Maltese, Suzy, under her arm, the dog all washed and beribboned. It silently lifted a lip at me in warning. I eyed it from a safe distance. Little Suzy was known as being a little shit when she was out on her own.

"Calm down, Mrs. Homas. Where are the birds now?"

She pointed a quivery finger over towards the oak tree.

"Around there! It destroyed my back yard, destroyed it I tell you! I'm going to the town about this! We need protection against people like him!"

I gave a mental eye roll. She was prone to hysteria, even under the best of circumstances. I could imagine her reaction to finding a bunch of Rhode Island Red hens scratching up her yard. I did my best to soothe her.

"It's alright, ma'am. I have it handled. Why don't you go inside and I'll take care of this?" I pulled out a couple of wire dog crates from the van, along with my big net. Mrs. Homas pointed at them.

"You can't use those! It will never fit in there!"

I looked down at the crate, the one I used for big dogs. Belatedly, I realized she was referring to the birds in singular.

"Ma'am, what kind of bird is in your yard? Dispatch said chickens."

"If that's a chicken, then I'm Angelina Jolie!"

She sure as hell didn't bear any resemblance to Angelina Jolie. My heart began to sink. "Well, what is it then?"

"How should I know? It's not mine, and it's tearing up my yard! I don't know what different kinds of birds are!"

I wondered if this was one of the turkeys.

"OK, let me go see what we got here then."

She trailed along behind me as I followed the little flagstone path around to the backyard, where the lawn opened up into even more gardens. A gazing globe in hues of blue dominated the center in a circular bed, red and yellow flowers nodding around it. The entire yard was flowering bushes, beds in neatly tended shapes, all defined by an emerald swath of lawn that meandered through it in a series of paths.

I stopped when I reached the end of the flagstones, taking in the tranquil oasis. My eyes tracked from side to side, taking in the birdhouses, a tiny pond with a waterfall, a purple butterfly bush coated with butterflies. No birds.

"Ma'am. Where was it?"

She was peering around me, Suzy clenched firmly under her arm. "I don't see it now! I was weeding my echinacea patch when this...this...thing suddenly appeared, right there! I was so startled and scared I just yelled and ran for the house as fast as I could! Poor little Suzy was terrified of it!"

'Poor little Suzy' gave me another silent sneer with her upper lip.

I started to walk towards the patch she had indicated, purple, heavy headed flowers bobbing in the breeze. "Well, whatever it was, I think it's..."

Suzy gave a barking snarl and kicked her way out of Mrs. Homas's arms. I caught a flash of gray behind the flowers as the dog streaked past me towards it, barking frantically. Mrs. Homas began to shriek, adding to the cacophony.

I stood and gaped as the long neck rose above a bed of cosmos, a fuzzy grey head topping it. There was a pair of big beady eyes over a wide brown beak. Suzy stopped short, barking hysterically while backing away. The head tilted, regarding her a moment, then lowered as the emu strode gracefully out from behind the garden, stalking towards the little terrier, whose barks were getting shriller.

"Oh, hell!" Apparently, at least one of the 'other' was an emu.

Suzy had backed up to the still shrieking Mrs. Homas, who scooped her back up, clutching her tightly as the bird advanced another step towards her.

"Mrs. Homas! Get in the house! Now!" I didn't like the way the bird was pinning them with that unblinking stare.

This time, she listened to me. She turned and scampered up the stairs into the sunroom that overlooked the lawn.

Leaving me alone with the biggest dang emu I had ever seen.

Now what?

I leaned my net up against the house. That wasn't going to help me. The bird and I regarded each other thoughtfully.

"Here, birdy, birdy, birdy." I held out my hand to him, palm up and cupped, as if I had something good. He stared down at it, taking a step towards me.... and pecked at my hand, hard. I yelped as his beak pounded into my palm.

"Damn!" I backed away a step. He advanced, puffing his stubby wings out from his body. Ah damn. This didn't look so hot. My palm throbbed from the impact of his beak. Behind me, I could hear Mrs. Homas still shrieking, mercifully muffled by the glass.

The emu advanced again. I retreated another step, my heel hitting something slippery and raised, putting me off balance. Stumbling slightly, I saw the emu puff his body out again as I glanced down, taking in the coiled garden hose I was standing on.

Hey....

I kept my eye on him as I bent down and groped for the hose, my fingers curling around a slippery shape. The emu stopped and watched intently as I pulled the hose up through my hand. I coiled it into a loose length of loops, one loop separated out and held in my right hand, the end trailing back to my left. He bobbed his head and tilted it again, regarding me. I carefully held my hand out with the single loop in it, steeling myself. "Here, birdy, birdy, birdy. Come here, my feathered friend."

He puffed up again and lashed out at my hand, but this time I was ready for him. I snapped my hand up, dropping the loop of hose around his neck as his beak missed me cleanly, then drew the loop tight with a snap. It closed down around his chest, not the neck, like I had hoped.

And all hell broke loose.

I had no idea these things were this strong. He leapt up in the air, his claws narrowly missing me as he raked his feet at me. It jerked me off balance, a death grip on the slippery hose. He leapt up again, yanking me towards him, pulling me right into his chest as the hose slipped free. In desperation, I grabbed him around the base of his neck, setting off a wild gyration of his head and neck, lashing around from side to side, pulling me off balance even more. His little wings pummeled the air, banging into my face and arms, sending stars across my vision. Dimly I could hear Mrs. Homas shrieking, Suzy barking shrilly. His neck cracked across the bridge of my nose, a white explosion of pain. The long legs were a blur, ripping at my side, sharp lancing pain searing through my body. I had to get this thing under control! I kicked my right leg out and over his back, pinning him under me. He dipped under my weight as I wiggled my leg further across him.

I felt his body under my legs, pulsing as he tried to free his stubby wings. I shifted my weight to the right, clamping down over the other side, changing my grip on the base of his neck, slowly working my way up. My feet lifted clear of the ground.

Oh hell!

The emu spun around in circles, his neck and head lashing as I clung to his back, fully astride him now, clinging like a monkey to his neck. He stopped spinning abruptly. I gasped for air, shifted my weight, trying to get a better grip on him...and he took off in a dead run.

Bushes crashed around us as he tore through the butterfly bush, made a sharp left turn at the trellis covered with morning glories and ran full tilt across the center of the lawn again. I caught a glimpse of my bloodied face reflected in blue hues in the gazing globe as he tore over it, the glass popping like a giant bubble. The bird was frantic now, making bleating sounds as he weaved and thrashed through the cutting flower garden in front of the sunroom. I saw the glass wall looming in front of us and steeled myself for the crash.

He hit it hard, slamming my forehead into the glass, and crumpled to the ground, stunned. Mrs. Homas came running outside, screaming unintelligibly at me, Suzy loose and racing alongside her. I clung to the emu's neck as Suzy barked and snarled inches from my face, shouting at Mrs. Homas.

"A rope! A rope! Get me a rope!"

"I don't have a rope! You just destroyed my garden!"

"Dammit, I don't care! Get me something, anything that I can tie him up with before he comes too!" He was starting to twitch again.

She finally realized that he was waking up. "I...I...well... here! Use this!" She disappeared back into the sunroom, emerging with an extension cord, still plugged into a lamp at one end. I grabbed it and started trussing the emu as fast as I could, Suzy snapping at my hands. Blood trickled down my lips, a brassy taste.

Breathing raggedly, I tied off the extension cord. The bird's legs and wings were now snugly trussed into his body. His eyes fluttered as I sat back on my heels.

"Well." I said.

"Well? Well? That's all you have to say is 'well'? Young lady, I am complaining to the Mayor about this! You just destroyed a third of my garden! I'm writing to the Board of Health! This thing is a menace! I want satisfaction!"

I rolled upright and tuned her out. I need to get the heck out of here, and fast. The emu's eyes had opened now, his beak open as he gasped for breath. I carefully slid my arms around his body and lifted. He was heavy, probably close to eighty-five pounds. My knees buckled as I rose, Mrs. Homas's grating voice adding to the ringing in my ears. I felt a tug as Suzy worked herself up for an assault, snapping at my leg.

I stagger shuffle hopped around to the van; the lamp banging against my thigh as the emu started to struggle again. Suzy was latched firmly onto my right pant leg, Mrs. Homas berating me all the way.

I wondered if Courtney ever had as much fun as this.

Chapter Seven

Uncle Jim was on the phone in dispatch when I came limping in an hour later. His eyes widened in shock at the sight of me. My nose was swollen, and my right eye turning black. The emu had also torn my pants from knee to ankle. I caught a glimpse of myself in the reflective glass in front of the dispatch office; leaves were tangled in my hair, dirt smeared across my forehead.

He hung up the phone. "What the hell did you get into now?"

"Your damned 'other' turned out to be a whopping big emu named Harry."

"An.... emu?"

I peeled a wad of dead leaves out of my hair. "Yeah. An emu with a temper."

Bobby Beleeno had been stunned when I dragged 'Harry' out of the back of the Paddy Waggin'. He was standing in the bed of his pickup truck, unloading bags of grain. Apparently 'Harry' had gotten impatient waiting for lunch and had taken it upon himself to go looking for it.

"Damn, girl!" Bobby was a short, dark complexioned man with stubby legs and long arms. "What the hell were you doing wrasslin' that thing? That's one bad ass bird!"

He had stopped short then, frowning. "Hey.... is that a lamp hanging offa him?"

I looked at Uncle Jim. "I told Bobby I was going to fine him if that thing gets loose again. And that he needed to go fix Mrs. Homas's garden."

Uncle Jim looked me over. "You up for another call?"

I groaned. Some days we had nothing. Other days, all hell broke loose. This was starting to look like an 'other' day.

"What now?" I took the sheet of paper from him.

"Martha Cooper called, all upset. Her dog is missing. Wants you to come out and take a report on it."

I scanned the sheet. "A Cockapoo? We haven't had any reports of any small dogs loose. Just that big one I went on earlier, over to the Meadows."

"Any luck?"

I shook my head. "No. I checked out the area, but there was no sign of him. I'll keep looking over that way, see if he turns up. Oh, hey.." The thought struck me. "Do the Addison's have an ox?"

Uncle Jim wrinkled his face up at me. "An ox? I don't think they have anything like that."

"Well, someone has some sort of mammoth white steer over there. I saw it twice. It's up in the woods near the tracks. Had an eye on it this big. I'm telling you, that thing was as big as a moose!"

"Huh. I hadn't heard anything about it. I'll ask 'em tonight."

The dispatch phone went off at his elbow. "See ya." I waved at him as I left.

Martha Cooper was waiting for me when I pulled in. A large woman, she was wringing her hands, her mouth working in anxiety. Her hair was haphazardly piled on her head, a long tunic came down to her leggings clad knees. A pair of Crocs completed the look.

"I KNOW something happened to my dog! I just know it! What are you going to do about it?"

I pushed the door of the Paddy Waggin' open with a creak. "Ms. Cooper, let's not get ahead of ourselves here. How about you tell me what happened?"

Tears leaked from the corners of her eyes. Oh heck...

"Fancy Nancy NEVER goes anywhere without me. Never. I know someone stole her!"

"Ma'am, we may have a lot of things that have happened around Brownville the past couple of years, but we never really have people stealing things, least of all dogs. Now, are you sure she hasn't gotten locked in someone's garage or something?"

She shook her head, tears coursing down her cheeks. "No! She never leaves the porch unless I take her. She's been with me six years and this is the first time she's ever not been there when I go to let her in."

That didn't sound good. With a sigh, I listened as she recounted the details of the afternoon leading up to Fancy Nancy's disappearance.

With difficulty, I extricated myself from her some forty-five minutes later, most of which were spent repeating what she had already told me.

My cell phone started ringing as I escaped to the Paddy Waggin'. The Brownville Police Department dispatch number came up.

Uncle Jim was on the line. "Uh, Rachel, you gotta get over to Barton Lane. The Dewall's dog is missing. Just plum disappeared about two hours ago."

I groaned.

If I could have murdered Roger at that moment, I would have.

Chapter Eight

Amanda plunked down my tea on the stained plastic table, slopping some over the side in the process. I held my phone against my ear, scribbling down the message from the voice mail. I smiled my thanks at her.

She blew carefully on her cup, flipping blonde hair back over her shoulder. "Thanks." I said, as I turned my phone off.

"What is it this time? Someone's dog pooping on a neighbor's lawn?"

"Naw." I sipped the scalding brew. We were sitting in the food court of the Riverdale Mall, one of the few places we had available for a Friday night movie get together. "Well, close, sorta. That's another call about a missing dog."

"Another one?" She placed her cup down and rummaged in her bag, pulling out a chapstick. "How many are missing?"

"This makes three calls in the past week. It's odd. We never have anything like this, and suddenly there's three in one week."

"Are they turning up?"

"Not so far. And I've scoured the town looking."

"Huh. You think someone is stealing them? I read about that happening a lot in the cities. They resell them on Craigslist for a couple of bucks."

"I dunno. All I can tell you is it's weird. The Chief is really upset about it. One dog belongs to his neighbor, so he's hearing about it daily."

"He still bent about the K of C Hall?"

I groaned. "Yeah, you could say that! Fortunately, they decided not to make a fuss over it. Seems the fire marshal ruled it as accidental, so they are looking to get a decent insurance payout. Guess they've been wanting to remodel that place for years." I gave her a rueful smile. "They told me they were looking to add a billiard room. He said they would name it after me."

Amanda coughed on her tea. "Oh my God, that's awesome."

"Yeah, awesome..."

She giggled. "No, seriously! You'll be the first one from our class who has an actual room named after her!"

"Why am I underwhelmed at this?"

She looked at me for a long moment. "How are you doing about Roger?"

His name sent a spear through my gut.

"Fine! Couldn't be better!"

"Liar." She took a sip of her tea.

I traced a drop of tea on the table. "I called him Tuesday."

"Why the heck did you do that?"

I shrugged. "I guess I just wanted to tell him about everything that's been happening. You gotta admit, it's been a crazy couple of weeks." I hadn't spoken to him or Skyped him since the night before the emu wrestling match, almost two weeks ago now.

"And?" She rested her chin on her fist.

I felt the burn in my gut as I thought of his reaction. "He was.... polite."

"Polite? Since when has Roger ever been polite?"

I grimaced. "Yeah, I know, right? Sounds like he and Courtney are really getting into each other. He kept talking about 'they' this and 'they' that."

"Jesus, Rachel! Cut him off! Lose his number, block him on TikTok, Facebook, Twitter; all of your social media! You did unfriend him, right?"

I shook my head. Not only had I not cut him off, I was spending hours at night trolling his page. I found myself poring over at the ever-increasing batches of photos he was putting up of himself and Courtney. I flipped through posts as they toured London, dined at quirky pubs and posed together at Stonehenge. It was a savage game I played with myself.

She sighed. "Girl, you are just torturing yourself. Stop it! Look, Patrick has a guy he works with who is kinda cute. Why don't you come over tomorrow night for pizza and we'll invite him too? I think you might like him!"

Oh geeze. Now I was the spinster friend, being invited over on a blind date. No way!

"Thanks Amanda, but no. I have plans."

"Really? What kind of plans?" She folded her arms and pinned me with her dark eyes.

"Whoops!" I looked at my watch. "Movie's gonna start in five minutes. We better get going!"

She stood up and gathered her things. "Chicken."

Chapter Nine

"There's a goat with an 'apparatus' on its head over
on Merry Street."

"A...what?" I scanned the report. "An 'apparatus' covering its head? What the heck is this?"

Uncle Jim shrugged. "Guess you'll find out. Better to be on the road today, anyway. Chief's on the warpath about the missing dogs. Think I'd stay outta the station for the day if I were you."

"Great." This Monday was starting out on a bad note.

My stomach churned, a sour mix. Uncle Jim looked at me. "You sure you up for this? You can take the rest of the day after this one if you need to. Billy can cover the animal stuff."

"No. I need the money." This job paid a pittance for being there, and a 'commission' for every call they actually sent me out on. I needed every whack job call I could get.

Uncle Jim nodded. "Call if you need help this time, okay?"

Merry Street was misnamed. It dipped down behind the train tracks, where a collection of sagging houses sprinkled with moldering trailer homes lay. They were bracketed with yards sporting a collection of derelict automotive memorabilia. Chicken coops and pens made of pallets lined the back yards on many of them.

I creaked and bounced to number 18, a graying white single story home set near the end of the street. In contrast to some residences on this street, this one had no rusting hulks in the side yard. It did sport a collection of mythological creatures welded from an assortment of scrap. A horse made of car suspension pieces pranced along one side of the lawn, a turkey made with old rakes and lawn implements on the porch. Ned Brothers lived here, an 80-something confirmed bachelor, the creator of those weird lawn art pieces.

The porch creaked under me as I climbed the single step to knock. The door swung open, revealing a dim interior and what looked like a gnome.

He barely came to my chin. He peered into the bright daylight, filmy eyes squinting.

"Hey Mr. Brothers. I'm here about the goat?"

"Eh? Who is this? My eyes aren't what they used to be, you know."

"It's me, Rachel, Rachel Tillison."

"Oh, Rachel. How's the family?"

"Good, they're good."

"What are you doing here? I was waiting for Joe." He scratched a stubbled chin, frowning.

"I'm the animal control officer now. Joe quit."

"Eh? Quit? When?"

"Couple months ago. Say, where's this goat?"

You couldn't get Ned to go any faster. His forefinger left his chin and wandered up to his left nostril, where it circled gently. I tried not to stare.

"Eh. Quit. Well, what d'ya know. Buster finally got the best of him."

"Eh?" It was my turn to use that word. "What are you talking about? Who's Buster?"

He ignored my question. "Rachel, eh? Marty's daughter?"

"Yes, Mr. Brothers. Now, this goat...?"

"I heard you were up north, in school. That you were getting married. You married now?"

There it was. That punch in the gut again. Damn you Roger.

"I uh, I'm out. Graduated last spring. I'm, uh..."

"You here about this goat or not? I ain't got all day."

Saved by senility.

"Where is it?"

He opened the door wider, releasing a stale, musty smell. "He's around back. Found him out there this morning. I think it's Buster, but I can't tell for sure."

Who the heck was 'Buster'?

He waved towards the back lawn. "He was back there a little while ago. Go on down and help yourself."

He gave a phlegmy chuckle as he closed the door in my face.

Chapter Ten

Ned hadn't cut his lawn since last spring. Grass whisked against my legs as I made my way around his house, cautiously peering around the edge of the back wall to look into the yard.

In the middle of the overgrown back lot stood a large black and white goat with a metal container on its head.

"Aw, what the heck is this?" I strode towards it, trying to make sense of what I was seeing. There was a muffled bleat from inside of what appeared to be an empty, partially rusted out metal drum of some sort. The thing was just large enough that the goat had wedged his head and horns inside of it, effectively trapping him.

"Settle down, son. We'll get you out in no time." Confident now, I casually approached the goat and wrapped an arm around his neck. Another harsher bleat sounded from inside the can.

"You better be careful there, Missy!" Ned had opened the rear window, his finger still tracing circles around his nostril.

"I got him, Mr. Brothers. Looks like he just got his head

stuck in one of your cans here." I grabbed the edge of the drum. "I'll just pop this thing off and find his home. He live around here?"

"That there is Buster, Missy. I can see them markings on him now. Whatever you do, don't let go a' him!"

I was tugging the drum free of his head as Ned yelled that. "What...?"

The goat exploded into the air. "Whoa! Hey! Hey now!" I held on to his neck for all my might as cloven feet flailed past my face. He was strong...and he stunk to high heaven. I heard Ned's phlegmy laugh again. "Whoo eee! Ride 'em Cowgirl!"

"Shit!" The devil beast had managed to whip his head around, slamming one horn squarely into my midsection. My breath whooshed out as I lost all the strength in my arms and my tentative grip on Satan.

Bucking, he leapt away from me, every hair on his back standing straight up. He stopped suddenly, fixing slit pupiled eyes on me.

"You better run, girl! Buster's gonna gitcha! Hee hee hee hee hee!"

The goat lowered his head and reared up, launching himself at me. I slammed the empty can against his head, slowing him momentarily. Too bad it also pissed him off more.

He made a sneezing sound and reared again, driving his horned head at my face. I was busy running backwards, fending him off with the can. Around a pile of junk we went, him forward, me in reverse. Sweat stung my swollen eye as I batted and swung at him, Ned's cackling grating my ears.

With a huge "Chuff!" Buster the Devil goat made an enormous lunge, slamming past my weakening defense and head butting me to the ground. He leapt across my body, leaving hoof shaped bruises on my thighs as a memento. I lay there gasping, the sky slowly whirling. It felt like I had just been run over by a dump truck.

What the hell was that thing doing running loose?

Ned shuffled to my side. "Hey. You getting up? He's gone now. He don't hang around once he's schooled you."

"What is that thing? Jesus!" I sat up slowly, still woozy.

"That there is Buster. Summabitch been running loose in this neighborhood for pert near three years now. Joe got fed up with him. I reckon that's probably why he quit." He pulled a cigarette out with shaky hands and lit it, triggering a minute long coughing spell.

"Jesus! Couldn't you have warned me about him?"

Ned shrugged, picking a bit of tobacco off his lower lip. "You're one a' them college graduates. I figgered you'd know all about it yourself."

I glared at him.

"You better get used to it, Missy. This here is Brownville. We got our ways."

"Mr. Brothers, I grew up here!"

"Well then, you should know all about it, hey?" He gave a wide toothless grin.

I was beginning to think I didn't know much about anything at all.

Chapter Eleven

My phone started ringing as I hobbled back to the Paddy Waggin'. I dug it out of my back pocket in a shower of dirt compliments of Buster the Devil Goat.

It was Uncle Jim.

"Hey, you better get back here, pronto."

"Why? What's wrong now?"

"Chief's asking for you and he's got the Mayor here. I don't know what's going on, but she's looking pretty upset."

Uh oh. My heart started sinking.

"Okay. Be there in ten or less."

"Alright. Hey, you find that goat?"

"Yeah, I sure did. Why didn't anyone warn me about Satan?"

"Satan?"

"Yeah, Satan. Also known as Buster."

Uncle Jim snorted, "Oh shit! That was Buster?"

I sighed." Sounds like everyone knows about Buster except me! Yes, that was Buster, thank you very much!"

There was a muffled sound on the line that sounded

suspiciously like a laugh. "Aw shoot, Ah forgot all about him. You okay?"

"Yeah, more or less."

"Good. Get your butt back here, then. Uh, you don't need to go change your clothes or anything first, do you?"

I looked down at my dirt caked pants and hung up on Uncle Jim.

It took me closer to twelve minutes to get back to the station. I smoothed my hand over my clean pants I had snagged on the way past my house. If I had many more days like this, I was going to have to invest in another uniform.

I found the red Volkswagen Beetle that Mayor Bruce drove parked haphazardly across the handicap spot as I wheeled into the police station. My inner alarm bell began to go off.

Uncle Jim was in the hall when I entered the lobby. "Come on." He took off, me hobbling behind him. He looked over his shoulder at me. "Aw geeze. Now what happened to you?"

"Buster left his mark on me." I had two bruises shaped like hoofprints on my thighs. Uncle Jim shook his head. "Sorry Rachel. I just plum forgot all about him."

Somehow, that didn't make me feel all that much better about it. I followed Uncle Jim down the stairs to the lower level where the offices were, wondering what else there was about this job that people had forgotten to tell me.

Mayor Molly Bruce was pacing agitatedly around Chief Tony Santo's office, her arms folded tightly across her chest.

"There you are!" The Chief pushed back from his desk slightly as we entered, a deer in the headlights look on his face. Molly stopped pacing and whirled around to face me.

"You!"

I backpedaled. "Uh, yes ma'am. Uh, what can I do for you?"

She was a tiny woman, all wizened skin and a helmet of white, closely cropped hair. She barely came to my chin, and right now she was at my chin, glowering up at me. I tried to back away slightly, wondering if this was about my burning down the K of C Hall.

"Why aren't you doing your job, young lady? I told Tony I had my doubts about putting such a young thing in this position, but he assured me you could do it! Well, now I'm not so sure!" To my horror, she burst into tears.

I was speechless. Beside me, Uncle Jim stepped forward and took her arm gently. "Come on now, Molly. Set down a minute and get yourself together here. What seems to be the problem?"

Tears were streaming down her face. She wiped her arm across her nose, leaving a glistening trail on her sleeve. "Mr. B-b-bones is m-m-missing."

Mr. Bones was her Yorkshire Terrier, a little tan lap dog who went everywhere with her. My stomach sank.

"What? Mr. Bones? But how did that happen? He's always with you!" I frantically tried to figure out where he could have gone without her knowing. The sad answer was; nowhere.

"I let him out in my backyard to do his business a little while ago, and when I went to let him back in, he was gone."

"Could he have wandered off?" Uncle Jim asked her.

"No! I have a fenced-in yard! The gate was closed and locked still."

I thought for a second. "Could he have dug a hole under the fence? Wouldn't be the first dog to dig his way out."

Again, she shook her head no. "No holes, no open gate, fence is too high for him to jump." She shuddered, her lip quivering. "Someone s-s-stole my d-d-dog!" And burst into a wail.

Chief Santos pinned me with a look as he crossed around his desk raising a hand to awkwardly rub her arm. Her sobs grew to a crescendo.

"Molly, it's okay, don't worry. Rachel will have Mr. Bones back before dark today."

What? How the heck was I going to do that? We already had three other dogs who had disappeared without a trace. Now I was supposed to guarantee the return of this one?

"Will s-s-she? W-why should I b-b-believe that?" Apparently, Molly had the same doubts as I did.

"Because I'll make sure it happens. I will spare no resources." He looked up at me. "Well? What are you waiting for? Go find Mr. Bones!"

His look said, "or else."

Chapter Twelve

The sun was setting.

I sat and stared at it through the windshield as exhaustion seeped through my body. Ordinarily, I would enjoy the reds and golds as the earth tilted away from the sun yet again. But tonight, with the Sword of Damocles hanging over my neck, I could muster no enthusiasm.

Eight hours spent searching for Mr. Bones without so much as a pile of dried poop to show for it.

It was impossible for a little dog to disappear so completely. Mayor Bruce lived in a close knit neighborhood; everyone there knew Mr. Bones. It would have been unlikely that he could simply leave and not be seen, if not picked up and returned, by someone.

Amanda's comments about dogs being stolen and resold echoed in my head. Frowning, I picked up my phone and dialed her number.

I got her voicemail and left a message asking her to work her computer magic and check the town's tax records for me. Maybe I could find out who lived in the area that way. Then, I disconnected and thought some more. Eight hours of searching, not just by me, but also from the guys on patrol, and nothing.

Nothing on the other missing dogs, either. Not a single sighting, not so much as a glimpse. It was pretty damn strange alright.

And out of character for Brownville.

I opened my notebook on my thigh and made a list of the addresses the missing dogs had all come from. It formed a rough triangle, some two miles wide. If someone was taking them, would it make sense that their location would be some place within that triangle? I tapped the pen against my front teeth as I considered this. There weren't all that many streets in the area. Mayor Bruce's home was on the outer edge on one side, a tangle of old residential streets, mostly named after trees. Inside the triangle proper, the streets thinned out to maybe half a dozen, most with large swathes of woods and fields on them. I traced my finger down Bollinger Street idly. You know....

I fired up the Paddy Waggin' and headed north.

Streetlights were flickering on in Mayor Bruce's neighborhood as I trundled past her house, noting how every light was on. A gaggle of cars filled her driveway; her loyal friends come to soothe her as we searched for Mr. Bones.

Bollinger Street curved off into darkness. Crickets and katydids screeched as I crept along, the lights off in the van. Darkness pooled under the trees, starbursts of light through the branches from the houses speckled along the road. I was almost to Thatcher Street when I saw movement to my left.

"Hey!"

The black figure paused and then sprinted into the trees, several little scampering shapes around it. I hit the high beams on the van and swung towards the woods in a mad sprint, light carving across the dogs that were being pulled into the trees. I caught a glimpse of a brown Yorkie with a bewildered expression, alongside a Cockapoo who was refusing to go voluntarily. Locking the brakes up, I slammed the van onto the edge of the road and tumbled out of the door. "Hey! You there! Stop right now!"

The figure ran faster, dogs yipping and yelping in protest. The Cockapoo was actively fighting now, flailing like a caught fish. I closed the ground on them grimly.

A dog went wide of a sapling, hauling the fleeing person up short. I reached them just as they released three of the dogs and sprinted away again. "Stop! I need to talk to you!" Pounding footsteps through the trees was my only answer. In the darkness at my feet, a whimper. I felt around, finding one dog, then two. The third one was a rustle in the woods as it bolted.

"Shit! Come on kids, let's get out on the street and have a look at you."

The van was idling, lights streaking the trees. I hauled the dogs over into the illumination. "Oh, thank God!" Dirty, bewildered, and here, Mr. Bones stared up at me, tail tucked between his legs. Beside him, a little Chihuahua cross cowered, Colby, the dog belonging to Chief Santos's neighbor. I twisted around, looking back at the woods. Who the hell was that? And why did they have these dogs?

Chapter Thirteen

"I'm telling you, Amanda, it was the weirdest thing. Why would anyone have all of these dogs?"

"I dunno. I can't think of any good reason for it. I just think it's awesome that you found Mr. Bones in time. Holy crap, the odds of that were, what, like 100-1?"

I shook my head. "Probably higher." We were seated at the kitchen table in my house, mom and dad long gone to bed as the hour approached midnight. Jived up, unable to sleep, I had called Amanda about the night's adventure. She had responded with coffee cake and tea, the remnants which covered the tabletop before us. We sat and pondered in silence for a moment.

"Someone's stealing those dogs, but the question is, why?" Amanda drummed her fingers on the tabletop.

"I have no idea. And I have no idea who it could be, other than maybe someone in walking distance from where I spotted them."

Mayor Bruce had been speechless when she opened the door, but only for the briefest of moments. Her shrieks had split my ears as she scooped the wiggling Mr. Bones from my arms, Chief Santos looming behind her as she did. He made eye contact with me; I nodded towards the yard.

Her joyful shrieks followed us as we walked to the Paddy Waggin'. "Well, I owe you an apology, Rachel. I honestly thought you didn't have it in you. What happened?"

I had filled him in as I showed him his neighbor's dog. His eyes had narrowed. "Huh. I'll have the guys get on that in the morning then. There aren't that many people in that area. Good work."

"There's one dog still loose over there. I have to get back to try to find him. Can I get any help?"

He smoothed his cheek with a forefinger in thought. "Let me send Robert over there. He knows that area pretty well. You should get home and get some sleep. Tomorrow's gonna be a long day."

Sleep. Yeah, right. I kept hearing the rustle of leaves as the Cockapoo ran off through the darkness.

Amanda's voice broke my reverie. "You left me that message earlier about the tax records online. I have the site, but I haven't had a chance to look yet. You want to take a stab at it?" She glanced at the clock. "Or maybe we should wait. You have to be at work in 6 hours, and I'm due to clock in 9 hours from now. Here..." She rummaged in her purse, pulling a notebook out. "This is the site. If I get time tonight, I'll check it out too." She dropped the paper on the table.

"Thanks, hon. Maybe I'll check it out tonight then. I'm not very sleepy."

She eyed me for a moment. "Rachel, get your bad self off to bed right now."

I squirmed under her glare. That's the problem with good friends; they know your quirks a little too well.

"Yes, Mother." I replied. "Go home, Amanda. I'm going to bed now."

She frowned. "Why does it feel like you are full of shit?"

"Hey! Is that anything to say to your bestest buddy?"

"When that buddy is you, yes."

And damn if she wasn't right. Here I was, two hours later, stomping through the woods off Bollinger Street, Robert having given up and clocked off an hour ago. There wasn't all that much woods where I tromped, a thin scruff that divided two streets. My flashlight cut a pencil beam through the trees. Nothing, no white fur, no mysterious black figure, nothing but torn up ground like something had milled around here for a while.

I was in the area where the triangle narrowed, where Bollinger ran down to intersect with Plain Street. The trees had thinned out to a mere scattering here, the grayness between them marking the houses and lawns again. My light bounced over the churned up area, leaves kicked up and churned, dark mounds of varying sizes everywhere. I circled slowly, peering at the area closely.

It sure looked like something awfully big had been here.

Frowning, I straightened up and slowly turned a full circle, peering at the surrounding houses. In the slowly waning night, I could see large well-kept homes, expanses of fields running behind them. Far off, a dog barked, a lonely, echoing sound. Then, closer...a rustle. I froze.

The sound stopped, then started again, stealthy footsteps in the leaves. I held my breath, killing the flashlight against my thigh, waiting. The rustling moved away slowly, then strengthened again. I cocked my head. It didn't sound like a person. More like a dog, maybe?

Pursing my lips, I gave a soft whistle. "Hey boy, come here now."

The noise stopped.

I whistled again, "Here puppy, puppy, puppy, come on."

The rustling started again, heavier, faster, moving towards me quickly, with purpose. I heard a faint snorting sound. The hair on the back of my neck stood up.

"Shit!" I muttered, fumbling for the flashlight as the noise rose in intensity. My thumb slipped off the button, I grabbed for the light with my other hand to steady it. A beam of light shot out and bounced across the clearing...

"SHIT!"

Buster the Devil Goat stood not more than ten feet from me, every hair on his back erect. His slit pupiled eyes fixed on me as he tossed his horned head and made another, louder snorting sound. I jumped as the adrenaline dumped into my body in a rush, arms and legs suddenly shivering under it. Buster reared, a loud 'Chuff' coming from him, and charged.

I feinted left, grabbing a small sapling and spinning myself around it. He plunged past, making a scything motion with his horns at me as he passed in a blast of wind. Adeptly, he reversed direction, spinning around the sapling behind me, 'Chuff! Chuff! Chuff!' My feet scrambled for purchase, the tree whipped and bowed under my weight.

I lost my footing on the second pass, sending my head towards the ground, my hands wrapped in a death grip on the tree. Of its own volition, my right foot kicked out, catching Buster square on his nose. He made a strange bleating noise and stopped abruptly, shaking his head violently as he licked his lips. I slowly pulled myself up, my panting filling my ears. He turned his head and glared at me.

I swear his eyes glowed red.

This time, he didn't waste time making any noise. He bounced once like a pogo stick, twice with some reach and third time square into my midsection. I was in slow motion, frozen, unable to turn, move or avoid him.

The blow felt like a sledgehammer. My feet flew up as my head cracked backwards onto the ground. My last vision was of Buster the Devil Goat rearing up over me, readying himself to drive his horns into my face.

Chapter Fourteen

"Hold still. You still have dirt crusted in this cut." Mom was none too gentle about removing it as I squirmed on the toilet. In the kitchen, rattling sounds marked Dad's progress in getting the coffee poured and served. It felt like the time when I was ten and tried to take a shortcut through the pasture where the bull had been turned out. It was something she'd warned me of over and over. That time, my right leg had borne the brunt of it, and had undergone a cleaning about as gentle as this one.

She scrubbed harder on my scalp, her lips a thin line as she swabbed my head with Betadine.

"Mom......ow! Come on, that hurts!" I pulled away from her, tears prickling my eyes. "Why are you mad at me, anyway?"

She pulled away from me, dropping the swabs on the sink's edge. I looked at her in the fluorescent light, noticing how drawn her face was. Glasses rimmed bright blue eyes, her hair worn in short curls. When had it gone so gray? I realized with a start I'd been so wrapped up in my own world, I had paid little to no attention to theirs since I had come home.

"Mom.... what's wrong?" I put my hand on her arm, feeling the soft flannel of the threadbare robe she wore, one I'd given her a long time ago. She pulled away, biting her lip. "I don't like this job of yours. That's what's wrong." She pinned me with her laser glare. "You have a degree in Computer Science, a degree that cost almost as much as a house, I might add! When are you going to get a real job, instead of running around Brownville getting attacked by a damned goat?"

"Ah, Janet, cut her some slack." Dad stood in the doorway, cups of coffee held gingerly in both hands. He set them down on the sink. "At least she has some sort of job for now."

Mom straightened up, tears forgotten, chin jutting up. Uh oh...

"Slack? Slack? Cut her some slack, you say? Okay, Mr. Congeniality, of course I'll cut her some slack! Why, I think it's wonderful my child comes home with her head half caved in at 4:30 in the morning after we spent close to $60,000 to send her to that school for a degree she'll never use! Oh, you're right! It's just GRAND that she has this job, grand I tell you, grand! Better to have this than nothing at all!"

She pulled her robe tightly around her and stormed out of the bathroom past Dad, who stood there looking deflated.

"Geeze! What was that about?" My eyes stung as tears swam in them.

"Aw, honey, she's just upset that you got hurt. Don't take it to heart. You know how she is." He stood there, shirtless, the beginnings of a potbelly hanging over pajama bottoms, tousled brown hair and beard. I loved my dad, always had. He was my safe place, my shelter, when Mom's moods became mercurial. I reached for one of the cups of coffee, suddenly aware of how tired I was. And another shift beginning in less than two hours, too.

Dad took the other cup and sat on the edge of the bathtub. We sat in companionable silence for a moment, sipping the brew.

His voice interrupted my musing. "So, how much longer are you going to be doing this job? I thought it was temporary."

I realized with a start that I had already been on the job for almost three months now. "I...I don't know. When Uncle Jim offered it to me, he said it was until they hired a new full-time person. I just assumed that they would have done it by now."

With so much going on, and not to mention Roger's defection, one day had simply blurred into the next.

Dad made a non-committal sound in his throat and sipped. "Honey, if you're going to stay on, you had better sit down with them and get a genuine commitment, one with benefits. We've been carrying your insurance since you got out of school, and frankly, we aren't going to be able to do that much longer. Then there's the matter of the school note. I don't want to sound like your mother, but it's getting tight around here with that added to the mix."

I stared at him for a beat. Holy cow, I hadn't given so much as a thought to things like insurance, or loan payments. A flush started up my cheeks, my eyes prickling. Dad looked over at me. "Aw honey, don't look at me like that!" He patted my knee. "We'll get by. But it will help if you can settle down and get a better job, take up the responsibilities from us." He leaned over, a smile cracking his face. "After all, it's not like you graduated with a degree in dog catching."

Chapter Fifteen

y mood was as gray as the sullen sky. I stomped across the police station lot, my head throbbing with every stride.

No sleep, no money, and no Roger. But wasn't it nice that Roger and Courtney had gone off last weekend on "Daddy's" Lear Jet? Oh, such a cheery little jaunt they had! It was simply because there was room on the flight; they were scheduled to deadhead to the coast to pick up an executive. From the photos Roger had posted, they had stayed at a charming little B&B off the western coast, the sea crashing below the cliffs as Stonehenge sent long shadows over their beaming faces.

I desperately wished one of the monoliths would succumb to gravity and flatten them both.

This is what I got for stalking them online again. I didn't mean to, didn't want to. I meant to go online and un-friend him after Dad left me with a cooling cup of coffee in my hand. I was weighted down by the revelation that my parents were carrying so much of the financial burden because of me. Because of my preoccupation with my own life and my obsession with Roger's.

Time to cut ties, drop that load and move on; onward and upward. Dump him, then log on to Monster or Indeed and start a job search for a 'real' job. Right. On it.

I had the best of intentions when I logged on.

"One last look see, and off you go."

Oh boy...was that a mistake.

An hour later, my mind was filled with a depressed haze as I flicked over photo after photo of smiling faces, exotic places. I had logged out without deleting him, a fact I hadn't processed yet, except to acknowledge that this behavior wasn't me, wasn't the resilient Rachel Ann. This was someone I barely knew.

I flung the door to the station open.... and collided face first into someone's chest.

"Oh! Damn!" Stars sparkled across my vision as the impact whacked my Buster-damaged nose.

"I'm so sorry! Are you okay?" Hands grasped my upper arm, steadying me. I opened my watering eyes slowly to see light gray eyes under a shock of curly brown hair, a neatly trimmed mustache and goatee. He was young, maybe early twenties. I rubbed a hand over my cheek as my tongue momentarily seized up.

Smooth move, Rachel.

"I'm so sorry! Did I hurt you?" We both realized he was still holding my upper arms at that moment. His cheeks flushed as he released me quickly. I rubbed a hand over my shabby work pants self-consciously; I was down to wearing the hand-me-down uniform thanks to Buster.

"I'm fine, really!"

We both stopped talking. Oh, awkward much? I stepped to one side.

He opened his mouth, then closed it as his eyes scanned me. "Are you...Rachel?"

"Um. Who wants to know?" I winced inside as my snarky side poked its head out.

"You found my Aunt's dog, Mr. Bones. Wow! It's great to see you again!"

I tilted my head at him. "Mayor Bruce is your aunt? Have we met before?" I was pretty sure I would have remembered him.

"Yeah! I'm sure I know you. But from a long time ago, maybe 7th grade?" He cocked his head a moment, those pale gray eyes studying me closely. A flush started up my neck.

"Ah! I have it!" A long finger pointed skyward. Flustered, I stammered, "Wha.. what?"

A triumphant smile. "You were the girl who blew up the science lab!"

Oh geeze! Just once, once, you mix two chemicals in the wrong sequence and the entire world remembers nine years later. My shoulders slumped. "Yeah, well, um. Gotta go. Nice to see you..." That hadn't been one of my finer moments. I went to step around him.

"I'm Brian. Brian Metzger. I know you know me." He smiled at me, dimples and a flash of white teeth.

I halted. "Brian Metzger? Didn't you get suspended for dragging Kelly Flynmore through the mud during field day?" It was an epic moment. Kelly was 'that' girl; vain, wealthy (according to her) and ostentatious. On a muddy field day, the last week of school, Kelly had crossed Brian and his friends one too many times. In a fit of devilment I could only envy, they had tangled her in a soccer net and dragged her through the largest puddle on the grounds. She had looked like the loser in a mud wrestling contest.

Brian had left school that day and didn't return, not that week, not the next semester. I hadn't thought about him in years; he sure didn't look anything like the juvenile delinquent that I remembered either. I hadn't realized until just now that he had disappeared.

It was his turn to look nonplussed. "Yeah, uh, that was kinda mean. I felt bad about it."

I cocked my head. "Really?"

A mega-watt smile peeked out for just a moment. "Well, kinda. For a little while anyway. Hey! Aunt Molly said you're the Animal Control Officer in town now?"

I nodded, "Yeah, I am."

"Well, she's ecstatic that you found Mr. Bones. She thought he was gone for good."

To tell the truth, so did I. I found myself still oddly shy around Brian, so I mumbled, "Yeah, it was good to find him. Hey, gotta go to work now."

"Wait!" He reached out and put a hand on my shoulder. "Look, I'm around this weekend, and I really don't know many people in Brownville anymore. Do you want to go to Smitty's with me on Saturday night? I was thinking about catching dinner, maybe the game? You into that?"

It sounded a little bit like I was better than nothing, but what the hell. It wasn't like I had anything to do other than cyber stalk Roger, anyway. I gave a tentative smile. "Um, sure. I guess. That would be fine."

There was that smile again. When we were in middle school, he was a pale, gangly dork of a kid. I wondered what had happened to make him look like this.

"Great! See you there at 7:00 then?"

I nodded. "Okay, sure."

As he walked away, it hit me. Holy shit, had I just accepted an invitation for a date?

Chapter Sixteen

"Brownville ACO," Uncle Jim's voice crackled across the radio.

"Yeah, uh, I mean Brownville ACO copy."

I heard a chuckle over the line.

"Swing over to the station, would you? Timmy picked up a dog and none of us recognize it. We may have to have you go see Dr. Johanson with him, see if he's chipped or something."

"Copy that. Be there in 5."

The little Chihuahua stared sternly at me as I entered dispatch. Diana Masters swung away from her computer to regard him.

"Whoever this is, there are no tags or collar. No reports of anyone missing a Chihuahua. None of us recognize him; do you?"

I looked at the dog, who cowered back slightly in the basket they had placed him in, but still kept direct eye contact with me. I shook my head.

"I can't say I've met this guy before. Hey little one. What's up? Where are your people?"

I crouched down and held my hand out to him. He looked away from me, but kept a wary eye on me out of the corner of his eye. I was going to have to go slow with this one.

I gently looped a slip lead over his head. "Where was he picked up?"

Diana glanced at her screen. "Timmy found him over on Plain Street."

Close to where I had seen my mystery walker.

The dog came willingly as I started toward the door. "Is Dr. Johanson expecting me?"

"Yup. I called him about ten minutes ago."

"Good. And how is he today?" I had a good reason for asking that one.

Diana smiled slightly. "I think he's probably okay."

I rolled my eyes. "Probably. Okay, thanks."

I heard her laugh as I left the room. "Have fun!"

Doc Johanson's clinic was just off the center of town, where the city streets started opening back up into farmland. I wheeled the Paddy Waggin' into the dirt parking lot in a cloud of dust. The small concrete block one story hospital was painted dull brown and topped with a flat roof. Once a gas station, it had housed Dr. Johanson's clinic for some twenty years now.

I slid the door of the van open and the Chihuahua hopped out and surveyed his surroundings. His tail immediately tucked between his rear legs.

"I know, little man. You can smell a vet from a mile away." Even I could smell the distinct aroma a veterinarian's office held, a mixture of disinfectant and animals.

The bell above the door jingled as I entered the small wood paneled waiting room. Holly Jenks, Dr. Johanson's assistant, was seated behind a high walled reception desk, her workspace lit by a large plate-glass window that once looked out at gas pumps. Her hair was salt and pepper, cut short to curl on her neck. Reading glasses hung from strings around her neck and her butt spilled over the edge of the chair she sat in.

"Hi Rachel. I heard you had some excitement the other night." Holly was the mother of a high school classmate of mine, Anna Jenks. I had known her since kindergarten.

"I guess you could call it that, Mrs. J. I don't know what's going on around this town anymore."

She shook her head. "Me neither. I swear, it's like ever since last year when Sandy came to town things just haven't been the same."

"Well, it wasn't her fault," I replied. "Those creeps would have come to town no matter what."

"I guess. Still, I'm not used to this much going on here." She stood up and peered over the counter at the little dog.

"Who have we got here? I don't think we have seen you before, Little Man."

I shook my head. "None of us know who this is, either. We need to have Doc scan him." I glanced at the closed door to the exam room. "Um, how is he today?"

"Well...he'll be fine for this. I don't think it's too bad today."

"Okay. Hey how is Anna doing?"

Mrs. Jenks started filling me in on Anna's life since she left Brownville. The door to the exam room opened and a pair of watery blue eyes magnified by glasses glared out at me. "Next. I don't have all day here!"

I glanced around at the empty waiting room and the parking lot, which was empty save for my vehicle. Mrs. Jenks's mouth thinned slightly. "Coming, Fred."

Dr. Johanson fixed his baleful stare on me. "All right, young lady, let's... PICKLES... go."

I gave an internal eye roll. Dr. Johanson had a mild case of Tourettes, a condition that had flared up after his wife left him three years ago. By all accounts, he took it hard, really hard. Her defection had left the formerly quiet, mild-mannered veterinarian with a number of odd quirks he was helpless to control at times.

I followed him into the exam room, where he scurried around the table to the counter behind it. He picked up the chip scanner and set it down again. His thin shoulders rolled under his lab coat.

Carefully, I lifted the Chihuahua up and placed him on the table. His ears were back against his head and he regarded Dr. Johanson warily.

Dr. Johanson picked up the chip scanner and replaced it on the counter again. He ran a long-fingered hand across his thinning brown hair, then straightened his already straight bow tie. His shoulders rolled under his coat again.

Holly entered the room behind me. "You want me to scan this little guy, Doc?"

He turned and peered over his half glasses at her, his face angular and drawn. "That's quite al.. PICKLES...right Mrs. Jenks."

He picked up the scanner again and started to set it down, then stopped. With supreme effort, he turned and waved it over the dog from nose to tail. The scanner beeped. He peered at the window on it.

"PICKLES! He's chipped. Looks like with...ahem... Home...ahem...Again...ahem."

He waved the wand back over the dog. It beeped again.

"He's...ahem...chipped."

I shared a glance with Holly. Looked like he wasn't having a good day after all.

She gestured toward the door with her head. "We are all set, Doc. Come on Rachel. I'll call the company and see if they updated the info on him."

I followed her out into the reception area, glancing over my shoulder to see Dr. Johanson picking up and setting down the scanner again, his face screwed up in concentration. The door swung shut behind me, cutting off my view of him.

Holly grunted slightly as she wiggled her way back into her chair. She sighed as she lifted the receiver. "Such a shame. He's such a good man and a good veterinarian. Loretta leaving him like that just undid years of work he did to become successful despite having Tourettes."

I held the Chihuahua against my chest. I could feel him shivering slightly through my shirt.

"Is he getting any better?"

"He has days where he doesn't show any signs at all. It's all about concentration. If he is concentrating, he does great. When he is in surgery, he's relaxed, calm and focused. It's during the slow moments where he starts to unravel. Too much time to think about her, you know?"

Roger's face crossed my mind. "Boy, I know what that's like." I replied wryly.

The Chihuahua's name was Penske, and he belonged to Don Schumer, who had a home over in the north side of town. I frowned at that; Don was ancient, a widower who had lived alone for some ten years now. The fact he hadn't called in on Penske concerned me.

Penske was also lacking a rabies vaccine record. I called dispatch as I left the clinic and asked Diane to call Mr. Schumer about his dog.

I looked out across the road at the woods and thought about Dr. Johanson, the impact his divorce had clearly had on him. I felt a tic starting in my shoulder as I thought about Roger.

"Nope. Nope. Nope. Do not go there Rachel. Nope."

I turned the key and put the Paddy Waggin' in drive. "It's over. Delete him. Lose his number. Don't think about him ever again. You can do it."

Beside me in the passenger seat, Penske gave me a sideways look, his ears still back against his head.

"What? You don't think I can do it? Watch me."

Chapter Seventeen

I was glad Penske had gone home, freshly vaccinated and reunited with Mr. Schumer's housekeeper, who was looking after him while Mr. Schumer was up north visiting family. I was spared his judging look as I stared at my computer screen.

Roger had updated his status. "Spent the day hanging out with my honey at 30,000 feet. Welcome to the Mile High Club!" There was a row of winking icons after it.

181 people had "liked" it.

"You perverted little son of a bitch!"

"What?"

Officer Hill had swiveled around from his desk, fat jiggling over his belt. I diminished the Facebook page. "Nothing."

"You just call me a pervert?"

"No, I said you were introverted. You need to get out more."

He blinked at me slowly, then leered. "That an invitation?"

Ah geeze.

My extension rang. "Gotta go!"

The woman at the other end of the line cooled my enthusiasm for her call.

"This is Cheryl Puckarski calling. I demand to know what progress you have made in the search for my dog?"

Her Miniature Schnauzer had disappeared last Wednesday, leaving behind nothing but irate phone calls. "Sir Charles's" disappearance was another of a slowly growing list of dogs who simply had vanished. I traced lines in the condensation ring my Coke had left on my desk as she droned on in my ear. I really needed to banish Roger from my life. Now. And get a resume up on the employment sites. This was not how I wanted to spend my life.

Hanging out at 30,000 feet sounded like a pretty good way to live.

With a start, I realized Mrs. Puckarski had asked me a question. "Um, I'm sorry. What was that?"

She made an exasperated sound. "I said that you really should go over to Prudence Coolidge's house! I would bet that she has something to do with my dog disappearing! Everyone has said for years that she has issues! She has this 'rescue' over there, but she won't let anyone in to see the dogs. She's probably got our dogs over there too!"

"Ma'am, do you have any proof?" I doodled some more.

"Proof? That's your job! I want my Sir Charles back! I like how you managed to find Mayor Bruce's dog, but not mine!"

I broke the connection.

"Hey, Rachel." Officer Hill had turned back to me. I sighed. "What?"

He gestured at the radio. "Dispatch was just calling you. Something about a stray goose over on Forest Street."

I groaned. What were the chances this goose came from Bobby Beleeno's? I shuddered thinking about Harry the emu. I gave a heavy sigh and closed out the computer. Without deleting Roger. I'll do it tomorrow.

Chapter Eighteen

I slammed the door of the Paddy Waggin' shut, wincing as a puff of wet dog settled around me. In the back, an irate white goose hissed and clattered his beak unhappily from inside the dog crate I had unceremoniously shoved him into ten minutes ago.

I was headed over to Morton's farm, the dairy on the south side of town, where the adult Chinese goose had likely come from. They were the only people in town who had these distinctive looking geese, who peered straight up into the air like snotty society women, their beaks topped by a huge hump.

At least he hadn't tried to kill me as I corralled him.

Mrs. Puckarski's call bugged me. I knew Prudence Coolidge, had known her since I was a kid. She was always a strange woman, short, dark curly hair going gray, somewhat wall eyed. For years, she and her husband and kids had been fixtures in town, active 4H participants. Her daughter Kelly played soccer with me when we were both in 5th grade. She had always lived over in the big graying farmhouse off of Thatcher Lane.

Right smack in the middle of the area all of those dogs had been disappearing from.

I drummed my fingers on the steering wheel and thought about Prudence. Her husband had died some 5 or 6 years ago now. Sadly, Kelly had died in a car crash a couple of years ago, too. Her son, Jeremiah, had left town for college, and as far as I knew, had never returned. Prudence rattled around in the old house alone now, her dogs her only companions. I tried and failed, to recall the last time I had actually seen her around town.

News that she might be running a rescue over there wasn't good news either. I certainly hadn't been informed of it. I wondered how many dogs she might own now. Huh...I was actually the person in charge of that now, which meant I had access to the licensing records too.

I decided to drop off the hissing goose at Morton's and take a detour over to the Town Hall for a while. Looking up licensing records beat obsessing about Roger and the increasing worry I was feeling about seeing Brian Saturday night.

Morton's Dairy Farm sprawled along the banks of the Connecticut River. The meandering river marked the boundaries of his fields; his barnyard was a neat cluster of red buildings with two navy blue silos poking up to the sky.

No one was in the yard when I bounced in, the goose protesting in the back. Looking across the fields, I could see the tractors trundling along, chopped corn arcing through the air to land in the following dump truck. Harvest season was in full swing. I decided to drop the goose back in the fenced in pond area where the others paddled and chattered among themselves.

I opened the door and swung out.

I heard a "Thunk" that was so low frequency, so deep

and low the ear barely registered it. I looked around to see Tom, the massive white Tom turkey who was the patriarch of the turkey flock the Morton's kept, strutting toward me. He was puffed out in full display, his wingtips dragging in the dirt, his red snood extended to an impressive length below his beak.

"Oh, hey Tom." I pulled the side door open as he made another deep "Thunk" in his chest. As I leaned into the van, I could feel his chest bumping against the back of my calf. I leaned in and reached for the crate containing the goose.

I heard another "thunk" and felt him bump against my calf, harder this time.

I chuckled a bit. "Tom, knock it off, would ya—"

He had bumped into my calf again, this time hard. I felt his feet scramble on my calf as my knee folded forward under his considerable weight. He drove me down to one knee as he clambered up on my calf and began breeding my leg with alacrity.

"Oh, hey! Wait! What the heck, bird?"

His tail wagged back and forth and he made grunting noises, intent on his job. My knee was pinned on the ground, his feet were clenched in my pant leg.

"Oh, holy hell..."

I heard a truck motor pulling into the barnyard. Tom paid no attention to it. I looked up, red faced with embarrassment as Henry Little, Cyrus's farmhand, pulled in. He stared at me, round mouthed for a moment, speechless at the sight.

Tom remained focused on the task at hand. His tail waggled and his feet clenched in a death grip. I tried and failed to haul my leg out from under him.

From the truck, Henry finally found his voice. "Girl, what the hell you doing with that bird?"

"I can assure you, this is NOT consensual! Can you help get him OFF of me, please?"

Henry opened the door and lost his composure. "Oh, oh man, oh I just can't believe that bird! Ha ha ha ha ha!"

He sagged down against the door frame and clutched his stomach as he belly laughed. "Ah ha ha ha ha ha!"

"This is NOT FUNNY!" I tried again to drag my leg out. Holy cow, was this bird never going to finish?

With a final tail wag, Tom slid off my calf. He flapped his wings and puffed back out again.

Henry was in tears now.

I straightened my aching leg out, wincing at the mess on my calf that his claws had made.

Tom strutted over to the van and eyed himself in the side. He started gobbling and marching around it.

I glared at Henry. "Come get your damn goose out of my van, then!"

He wiped his eyes and straightened up. I heard a 'thump' on the other side of the van.

Cautiously, I peered around the back of it to see Tom puffed up and attacking his own reflection in the door.

Henry was still chuckling as he walked over to the van. I glared at him and climbed back inside to drag the crate over to the doorway.

"It was NOT FUNNY Henry!"

"You gonna report him to the police for assault and Butterball? Ha ha ha ha ha!"

He doubled over again.

"Shut up!" I could feel my cheeks flaming red.

Amidst the backdrop of Henry's laughter, I hauled the goose out and dumped it unceremoniously on the ground.

"Here! You can put him away!"

I clambered back into the van and cranked the starter

over just as my phone rang. I groaned. This day wasn't going all that well already.

I didn't know that it was about to get a whole lot worse.

Chapter Nineteen

ncle Jim's voice filled my ear as I answered the call.

"Hey Rachel, we got another missing dog. This time it's Mrs. Homas. Her little Suzy is gone. She let her out an hour ago and she disappeared out of her fenced yard."

I couldn't stop the groan that escaped my lips.

"Yeah, I know, but you better go over there and see her right away."

"What happened with the damage to her yard from Bobby Baleeno's emu?"

I heard something that sounded suspiciously like a chuckle. "The department's insurance is fighting with Bobby's insurance company over that one. Don't worry about it: if it comes to it, we'll swing by one night and clean it up for her."

Don't worry about it. Yeah. Right. I thought of little Suzy and her toothy disdain for me. That was one dog I could leave missing and have no guilt about it.

"Okay. Thanks...I guess. Hey, Uncle Jim?"

"Yeah?"

"Have they had any luck finding someone for this job yet?"

There was silence on the line for a moment. "Erm, I cain't say I know offhand."

"But they are looking, aren't they?"

"Why? What's up, Rachel?"

I sighed. "Mom."

"Oh."

Uncle Jim was Mom's brother. He, of all people, knew how she could get.

"Uncle Jim, it's just...well I need to have insurance and benefits. And a raise would help too. I have school loans to pay off."

The thought of sending that much money out for a piece of paper I wasn't using made me feel lightheaded.

"I hear you, Rach. Look, you think you're gonna stick around for a bit? I can talk to the Chief about getting you something more for what you're doing."

I sighed. "Uncle Jim...it's just...I didn't plan on coming back home. I thought I was going to go to Boston or LA and get a job coding."

"I know. Do you have any plans lined up yet?"

All my plans had involved Roger in one way or another. I felt the tears prickling the back of my eyes at the thought.

"No. No, nothing yet."

"Look, hang in there for a little bit, okay? Maybe I can have them hire you to help upgrade the computer network at the station too, use your skills and get some more money."

I slumped in the seat. "Yeah, sure I guess."

"I'll talk to him then. You better get going. Mrs. Homas is waiting for you."

Great. Just...great.

Chapter Twenty

Mrs. Homas was waiting in front of her house as I guided the Paddy Waggin' to a wheezing halt at the curb. And she wasn't happy either.

"You again! Why in the world did they send YOU to the scene of a CRIME? I want a REAL police officer!"

I resisted the urge to roll my eyes at her. "Mrs. Homas: I AM an officer. I'm the Animal Control Officer."

She snorted, causing her double chin to quiver. "Humph! More like an 'Animal Out-of-control Officer. Do you know I still don't have my yard fixed after that little rodeo stunt you pulled?"

Geeze, I got the dang bird out of her yard for her; you'd think she'd be at least a little grateful for that.

I pulled my notebook out of my back pocket. "Ma'am, why don't you tell me what happened? When did you last see Suzy?"

Her eyes filled with tears. "I let her out at exactly 9:45 for her mid-morning doody business."

I was scribbling as she spoke. "Eh? Her duty business?"

She waved a hand impatiently, "Doody, DOODY, you know, her BATHROOM break."

I scribbled, avoiding eye contact with her. Dogs didn't use bathrooms; why were humans always claiming they did? How come no one ever said they let them out to take a dump?

"Ok, so you let her out to...use the bathroom...a little over an hour ago now, right?"

Mrs. Homas nodded, looking across her yard. "She always wants to come back in within ten to fifteen minutes. She comes to the sliding door and barks once, just once, not twice."

She sniffled and swiped her nose.

"And you are certain the yard was secured? No gate left open? No holes under the fence?"

"Young lady, I am CERTAIN of that!"

"Alright, Mrs. Homas. I'm just trying to get all the facts. Now how long was it before you realized she hadn't come to the door?"

The tears that had threatened spilled over. "That's just it...I so rely on her inner clock, I just go about my business until I hear her! I had just started a quilt for my grandniece when I let her out. I was laying out the fabrics and planning it so I got wrapped up in it. Next thing I know, I looked up at the clock and realized it had been forty-five minutes since I let her out."

I jotted quickly in the book. "And then what happened?"

"I went outside and called and called for her. I thought maybe she got stuck someplace, so I started running around my yard, opening sheds and looking under things. But she was g-g-gone." A full-blown sob escaped her lips.

I did feel bad for her even though a small part of my

soul was happy to not be dealing with Suzy right that moment. Although now I was going to have to search high and low for her. The vision of the mystery dog walker crossed my mind.

What in the world was going on here?

"Mrs. Homas, are you absolutely CERTAIN there was no way in or out of the yard other than the gate?"

She nodded, setting off her jowls again. "I am dead certain of that!"

"Is there any way the gate could have opened accidentally, or not been closed all the way?"

"Absolutely not!"

I shoved the slim book back in my pocket. "Okay, ma'am. How about you show me the entrance to the yard, then?"

She jumped up and scurried around the front of the house to the fenced side yard. A solid white picket fence about four feet high surrounded it. Ornamental crabapple trees and flowering peach trees lined the fence from inside. She stopped in front of a solid gate with a black garden gate latch on it.

"Here. See this? Try to make the latch open accidentally or easily." She rattled the metal latch.

I thumbed the latch, noting the pressure I had to use to open it. The moment my thumb left the latch, the catch slammed down solidly. I tried it a couple times with the same result. Then I pushed the gate in and let go. It swung shut, latching firmly.

There wouldn't have been an accidental release with this gate.

I turned around so my back was to the gate and scanned the scene. Her yard bordered Molly and Bruce Mannion's yard. The side of their house was some 20 feet away, their driveway leading to the garage that stood close to the picket fence further up the property line. I looked at the side of the house, an old three story Victorian. The back porch had an unoccupied glider swing and baskets of flowers on the railing. From the side, it had steps leading down to the driveway, toward the one-car garage...

My eyes snapped back to the back porch, situated on the side of the house. Above the stairs was a motion activated light. Hanging on the bottom of the sensor was a round, black object.

"Hey..." I walked toward the house.

Behind me, Mrs. Homas trotted along. "What? What?"

I looked back at her. "You see that thing on the light on the back porch? That looks like a camera."

She sniffed. "They have cameras everywhere! It's such an invasion of privacy! I was telling Martha..." Her voice trailed off as the implication finally sank in. "Oh!" was all she could say.

"Wait here, ma'am. I'm going to see if they are home." I strode across the driveway to the back porch. Peering closely, I could see the camera clearly, one of the new popular security light models. I climbed the three steps and rapped on the glass sharply.

Silence greeted me.

"They work during the day." Mrs. Homas called out. "They don't usually get home until after five."

I turned back to her. "Okay. Do you have a good relationship with them? If you ask, would they pull the footage for you? If we have to, I could get someone at the station to talk to them, but it might be easier this way."

She shrugged. "I guess it's good enough. Molly likes to garden too, so we often share our tips and seeds with each other."

"Alright. So, you find that out, and I will do some searching for her. Leave the gate propped open and something of yours, like a sweater or a shoe out there for her. If she is loose and wandering, that may help her find her way back."

She nodded as tears slipped down her cheeks again. "I'll put my lap robe out. She likes to cuddle under it when we watch television together at night."

Chapter Twenty-One

Prudence Coolidge had a kennel license for 6 dogs. I scanned the property information quickly; two story home, built in 1929, one garage, 24 acres, 250' frontage on Thatcher Lane.

Closing the drawer on the records, I pulled up the animal inspection book Joe had last filled out. Squinting, I read his scrawling handwriting carefully. The dogs, a miniature donkey and a goat.

That didn't sound too bad. Six dogs were kind of a lot, but her house was big and she had a lot of land.

I closed the program out and pushed my chair back from the desk.

From across the room, Timmy Butler looked up from the report he was laboring over. "Uh oh. You look like you're on a mission."

"Yeah, kinda. I'm going to head over to Prudence Coolidge's. I'm hearing she might be involved in the missing dogs somehow."

Timmy snorted. "Wouldn't surprise me in the least. She ain't exactly been all there since her husband and kid died."

I felt a pang at that. I'd been so focused on the dog napping that it hadn't really crossed my mind why someone might want to do that. I recalled Kelly when we were in the fifth grade. A stout girl with unruly dark hair, she had been a tomboy and a natural athlete. Her death in an auto accident had come as an enormous shock to many of us in town.

It sounded like her mom most of all.

I heard the phone ring in dispatch. Timmy cocked his head, his fingers pausing on the keys of the computer.

In the dispatcher's cubicle, Diane Masterson put a hand to her ear as she spoke into the headset. She leaned over and looked into the room we were in, her lips still moving as she spoke with the caller. She made eye contact with me, raising one finger in a "wait" motion.

Uh oh...

Diane pushed away from the desk when her call ended. "Hey, Rachel, Tim, you guys gotta get over to Prudence Coolidge's place, pronto. She's claiming she was just terrorized by a giant white animal. Said it cornered her in her barn for the last hour She sounds pretty shaken up by what happened."

Timmy looked over at me. "Well, speak of the devil and up he jumps."

I stood up. "A 'giant white animal?' Did she say what it was?"

Diane shook her head. "Negatory. But she sounded pretty upset about it."

Timmy pushed back from his desk. "She ain't wrapped too tight, you know. This going to be another one of these stolen toast kinda calls?"

There had been numerous calls lately from one of the more unstable residents in town. Mostly complaints about breaking and entering that resulted in accusations of stolen toast and microphones planted in their toothpaste.

Diane shrugged. "I dunno. This is why they pay you the big bucks, Tim."

"Ha!" He hitched his pants up over his gut. "You ready to roll, Rachel?"

I grabbed my car keys off the desk. "I can hardly wait. Let's go."

Chapter Twenty-Two

The Paddy Waggin' thumped and creaked down the rutted driveway to Prudence Coolidge's house, following Tim Butler in his cruiser. I peered through the streaked windshield looking at her house, sad and sagging in the half gloom of the trees. The paint had defected long ago, leaving behind a brown and gray exterior on the two-story Colonial house, the porch sunken to the right of the door. A ramshackle one story shed clung to the left side of it. I could see furniture and boxes piled up in the upstairs windows, framed by faded curtains. The porch was piled high with boxes, empty dog food bags, buckets, tools and lumber. Behind the house, I could see the small barn at the back, the driveway ending at the door. I could see the bumper of a car in the gloom.

The entire thing was swathed in a coat of despair.

Tim pulled to a halt in front of the house and got out, adjusting his belly and plunking his hat on his head. I pulled in behind him and cut the motor. In the stillness, I could hear some crows making a racket behind the house. I climbed out and joined Tim.

He stomped up the creaking staircase and rapped on the doorframe.

"Mrs. Coolidge? It's the police."

From deep inside the house, dogs started barking frantically. I cocked my head, trying to pick out how many different barks I could hear.

"Jay-sus Ker-ist! How many dogs does she have now?" Tim eyed the sagging door with mistrust.

"The book says six." It sounded more like sixty. I was seriously beginning to wonder if there was truth to the thought that she might be behind the dog napping.

Tim rapped the door again, harder, the barking and howling drowning him out.

"Prudence, you alright in there? Answer the door or we're gonna come in!"

I looked at him. "Can we do that?"

"If she don't answer, we damn sure will. It's called ex-in-ge-ent circumstances."

"It's 'exigent' circumstances, not ex-in-ge-ent."

"If'n I say it's ex-in-ge-ent, then that's what it is, missy!"

"You can't just make up words!"

"And you can't tell me what to say!"

The door creaked as it opened an inch. A wide brown eye peered out at us. "Will you two shut up out here? I can hardly hear myself think over the noise you're making!"

Tim leaned toward her. "What? I can't hear you over those dogs!"

I rolled my eyes. "Mrs. Coolidge? It's me, Rachel Tillison. Dispatch said you were scared by an animal?"

The door opened a hair more. "Rachel? Lord have mercy, I haven't seen you in years now! What are you doing here?"

"I'm the animal control officer here in Brownville now, ma'am. We're here about the animal you reported."

Behind her, the barking continued, ear ringing in intensity. Tim rubbed his ears. "Can you come out here so we can hear you? How many dogs you got in there, anyway?"

The door opened slowly, revealing a slight figure draped in shapeless clothing. I was shocked at her appearance; she looked like she had lost 50 pounds since I had last seen her.

Glancing around nervously, she stepped onto the porch, pulling the door closed behind her. The decibel level dropped by half.

Tim shifted his weight, tugging his pants up to his belly again. "Mrs. Coolidge, what happened today? Dispatch said you reported a 'giant white animal'.

"Oh my gosh, it was awful! Terrifying! I've never been so afraid in my life!" Tears sparkled in her eyes and she wrapped her arms around herself, hugging her slight frame.

"What happened?" I eyed her body language; clearly something had happened to her.

She glanced around again, her eyes darting. "I was in the back when I heard something rustling. I th.. thought it was Luther. But it wasn't! It was this...this...thing! It was huge! And it charged at me! I had to run for my life!"

I shared a look with Tim, whose face showed pure skepticism.

"Who's Luther?" Tim asked her.

"Luther is my Walker Hound. He went out two days ago and hasn't come back. I was out back calling him when this thing attacked me!"

I wondered if that 'thing' was Buster the Devil Goat.

"Mrs. Coolidge, was there a chance this was a goat? We have a black and white one running loose around here and let me tell you this; he's pure evil."

She was shaking her head no. "I know what a goat looks like, and this was no goat! It was probably seven feet tall, for one thing!"

A chill snaked down my spine. "Seven feet tall?"

Beside me, Tim scoffed. "With all due respect, ma'am, there ain't no white seven foot tall animals around here."

Her face reddened. "I know what I saw, and it was a big, mean white animal! And it attacked me!" Inside the house, the crescendo of barking increased at her shrill tone.

Tim sighed and pulled his notebook out of his pocket. "Why doncha describe to me what you saw then? Any chance it was the Abominable Snowman?"

She wrapped her arms tighter around herself. "I don't need your lip! Get out of here!"

"Mrs. Coolidge, wait..." I put my hand on her arm. Tim shoved his notebook back in his pocket. "Rachel, you wanna talk to her, go ahead. I got things to do." He turned his back to us and tromped down the splintery stairs.

A tear spilled out of her eye. "Mrs. Coolidge, I believe you. I saw it too."

Tim stopped and turned back. "What? What are you on about?"

I glared at him. "I said I saw it too, over by the Meadows crossing. Well, not the whole thing, but I saw something white. And huge. It left tracks like a cow."

"Well, there you go then. I'm gonna bet Addison's have a steer loose again. Some of those things can be mean. Still ain't cause for concern, though."

I closed my eyes for a moment, biting my tongue. "Tim? How about you leave me be with Mrs. Coolidge and I'll get a statement, okay?"

He shrugged. "Knock yourself out."

Prudence sagged as he backed his cruiser around in the driveway. "I bet you people think I've lost my mind."

That was pretty much exactly what Tim had said, but I wasn't about to confirm it.

"No, no ma'am. They don't know much about animals, that's all. But I believe you because I saw it too."

She looked at me dubiously. "Really?"

"Yeah. Now how about you tell me what happened?"

She tightened her arms around herself. "I was out back, looking for Luther, when I heard this rustling and crunching noise coming from down in the gully. I started whistling for him, and suddenly the bushes started shaking!" A tear escaped her eye and rolled down her face, leaving a dewy track.

"Mrs. Coolidge, it's okay. There isn't anything here now." I patted her arm tentatively. She felt like bone wrapped in flesh.

She shook her head wordlessly as another tear escaped. "I...I know...I need a moment. I've never been so scared in my life!"

She took a shaky breath and continued. "I froze when I saw that. I mean, the only thing I could think of that could make the bushes shake like that would be a bear. But this was no bear! This...thing stuck its head out and glared at me! Then it came out of the bushes and started running toward me. It was making this hideous noise! I was so surprised I froze. Then it was right there, right on top of me! It was so big I had to tilt my head back to see it! I blocked the sun, it was so big!"

"Mrs. Coolidge; what was it? What did it look like?"

"I don't know what it is! I'm no animal expert! That's supposed to be your job! It was big, really big! It's snow white! There are no white animals in these woods: I'd know if there were. It had four legs and giant horns! It was making weird noises! And it was attacking me! I tell you what I did, Missy, I ran is what I did!" A sob escaped her lips. "I bet that...that thing killed my poor Luther too!"

In the house, the barking had slowed down to a dull roar. I asked her the question I had been pondering. "Mrs. Coolidge, you said you were looking for Luther. What happened to him?"

"I let him out two nights ago to do his business. He always takes ten minutes. Except this time, he never came back in. I've been searching and calling for him, but he isn't anywhere to be found! Someone stole or killed my poor Luther!" Fresh waterworks erupted from her eyes.

I patted her arm. "Now, don't jump to conclusions. We don't know, he could be locked in someone's garage maybe, got in there and they closed the door without seeing him."

She swiped an arm across her eyes.

"Mrs. Coolidge...can you show me where you were when you saw this animal?"

She nodded. "It was 'round back here, behind the house." Glancing around nervously, she stepped off the porch and threaded her way through a mound of fruit crates. Following in her wake, I looked around. The windows on the house were mounded with furniture and what looked like trash. Piles of dog poop littered the path, making the walk a feces filled minefield. Overgrown bushes scratched my pant legs. Water bowls, some empty and over-turned, glinted in the sun.

"Mrs. Coolidge, how many dogs do you have?"

She had stopped in the middle of the overgrown back-yard, the woods a dark, rustling border behind her. "Why do you want to know that?"

"I...uh, I was just wondering, that's all."

"Well, I have one less now!" Fresh waterworks steamed down her cheeks.

Aw geez.

"Okay, okay, so you were here when the animal appeared?"

She pointed at the wood line. "I was right there!"

I walked toward the hemlocks that ringed the massive oaks and ash trees. The ground was churned up. I saw a clear outline of a hoofprint, a two toed one like a cow would have. Leaning over, I placed my palm next to it.

It was larger than my hand.

I looked up at her. "Mrs. Coolidge, I don't know what this is, but it isn't an Abominable Snowman and it is real."

Chapter Twenty-Three

I leaned forward and peered at my lips in the bathroom mirror. Carefully, I picked a small fleck of toothpaste off the corner of my mouth. My dad appeared in the doorway.

"Are you still in here primping?"

I rolled my eyes. "I'm not primping, Dad. I'm just making sure I don't have spinach in my teeth."

"Looks like primping to me. Listen, are you done in here yet? Some of us need this room."

I sighed and stuffed a lip gloss into my pocket. "Yeah, yeah Dad. Here you go."

He shifted the newspaper under his arm. "So, who are you going on a date with tonight?"

"Brian Metzger, Mayor Bruce's nephew. And it's not a date, Dad. We're just hanging out together!"

"Looks like one to me. Come on now, out with you! And have fun, sweetheart."

I pecked him on the cheek as I passed. "Thanks, Dad."

Mom looked up from the kitchen table as I came downstairs. "Where are you two going tonight?"

I stifled a groan. "Nowhere, Mom. We're just going to grab something to eat and watch a game down at Smitty's Pub."

"Well, what time will you be back?"

"Mom! Come on, I'm an adult now."

"Last I checked, you are still my daughter and you are under my roof! So I need to know where you are going and when you'll be back."

I closed my eyes briefly and counted backwards from ten. "Yes, Mom."

Dad reappeared in the kitchen doorway. "Leave her alone, Janet. After all, it's not like she can go anyplace in town that we don't know about in five minutes, anyway."

"Geeze, you guys! Come on!"

Mom smiled and went back to her crossword puzzle. "That's true, Marty. And she had best not forget it!"

I snagged my bag off the back of the chair. "That's it! I'm outta here!"

"Have fun, honey." Mom called out.

"But not too much fun!" Dad added.

I let the screen door slap shut behind me in answer.

As I descended the porch steps, the butterflies kicked up in my belly again. Geeze, after everything I had done in my life, why was I getting these?

Brian's face flashed through my head. The butterflies kicked up harder.

Roger's face replaced Brian's, his eyes crinkled in amusement. I saw him the day we climbed Mount Monadnock, snow crunching underfoot as we hiked out of the tree line. Wind had tossed his hair across his left eye, his skin ruddy in the cold. I could feel his hand in my gloved one as we scrambled the last few feet to the peak.

I stopped at my car, my hand on the roof. The butterflies were gone, leaving behind a dry dust. Tears pricked at my eyes.

I didn't hear him until he spoke. "Rachel?"

I stiffened, swiping my eye surreptitiously. "Yeah, Dad?"

He placed a gentle hand on my shoulder. "GO! You owe it to yourself. And never mind your mom; if staying out until the wee hours makes you feel better, DO IT!"

I smiled as my eyes threatened to overflow. "Okay Dad. Thank you. I love you."

He hugged me. "And I love you too, honey. Now get on out of here!"

Chapter Twenty-Four

The door to Smitty's creaked shut behind me as the voices washed over me. I glanced around the room, about two-thirds full on this night. I waved to a couple of friends and spied Brian over at the dart board pitching darts while chatting with Sammy B., one of the owners of Smitty's.

I weaved my way over to him, noticing his broad shoulders under the grey linen shirt he wore. At some point, he had grown up, grown up a lot, actually. I noticed more than one female in the pub glancing at him.

Reaching him, I set my bag on the high top table and slid onto the stool. He glanced over at me and smiled, that megawatt smile he had.

"Hey." He greeted me.

"Hey yourself." I replied. "How are you doing?" I indicated the dartboard. "Sammy wiping the floor with you yet?"

Sammy stepped up to the board, a bunch of darts held in his left hand. He singled one out and took aim. "Not yet, but I'm about to."

Brian laughed and climbed onto the stool across from me. "He's going to have to bring his A game to the plate." He looked at me and smiled again. "You want something from the bar?"

"Sure. How about a Coke?"

"You got it. Be right back."

Sammy called over to him, "Better be quick. I'm about done with you here." He sent another dart flying with unerring accuracy at the corkboard. It thunked in a millimeter away from the first one that was seated firmly in the inner ring.

Brian shook his head. "I should know better than to try to hook him in a game of darts." He slid off the stool and made his way to the bar.

Sammy sent the last dart flying to thunk home in the bullseye. He grinned. "Yeah!"

I smiled at him. "He'll remember not to play you next time, I bet."

Sammy came over to lean on the stool next to me. Around mid-fifties with glasses and graying hair, he was a long time fixture here in Brownville. Sammy knew everyone, and Sammy saw everything.

He turned those all seeing brown eyes on me now. "How's it going, Rachel?" He glanced over at Brian. "I didn't know you were seeing Brian."

I blushed. "I'm not; we are just friends. I haven't seen him since like seventh grade now."

He watched as Brian grabbed our Cokes and started making his way back toward us. "I thought you were dating that guy from school anyway, what's his name?"

My stomach dropped. "It's Roger. And...no, no, we broke up a while back."

Sammy slid off the edge of the stool. "That's too bad for

him, but good for Brian. He always was a nice kid. Hey Brian!" He gestured with his head toward the board. "Too bad, kid. Maybe next time…or not. Have fun, you two!"

Brian groaned as he looked at the board. "Damn! I thought I had him."

"Well, the man practically lives here; he practices every day."

"Ha! Yeah, you're right. That's okay; I'd rather hang out with you, anyway. So how was your day?"

"Um. Okay. How about you? What did you do today?"

"Hey Rachel!" The voice came from my left. "I heard Thanksgiving came early this year! Ha ha ha ha ha!"

Looking over, I saw Dan Johnson and his best friend Carl, both old high school classmates of mine, both kind of jerks. Both kind of drunk.

And both employed at Morton's Dairy.

My face flamed red again. Brian looked at me in puzzlement.

"What's that about?"

"Nothing. Just work stuff."

Carl heard me. "Work? It didn't sound like work to me! Sounded like you had a good time. I know Tom did. He's been struttin' around since you were there all puffed up."

"Yeah, well, he was all puffed up before I got there, so that's nothing new."

Beside Carl, Dan had slid off his stool and pushed his chest out. He began strutting back and forth imitating a Tom turkey.

He looked ridiculous.

Brian was staring at them with one eyebrow raised. He looked at me. "You want to get dinner someplace else?"

"Oh God, yes, I'd love that!"

We slid off our stools and headed for the door. Behind

me, I heard Dan start gobbling like a male turkey. Looked like his turkey hunting skills were being used to humiliate me now.

The door slapped shut behind us, mercifully cutting off another round of gobbling. Brian looked at me wryly. "You want to tell me what that was about? Or would you rather skip it?" He opened the door on his car for me.

I flushed again. My first thought was to skip it, but what would that do? This was Brownville. If I didn't tell him, four more people would, so I gave him the condensed version of what happened.

His eyes were round when I finished. "Turkey's will do that? Like a dog would? Holy crap!"

I blushed, but I started laughing too. "Honestly, I was today years old when I learned that fact. Learned it the hard way too."

He pulled in to Dom's Pizza off Main Street. "This okay with you?"

"It's perfect." The butterflies were there again.

We sat in a booth overlooking Main Street, eating a meat lover's pizza and talking. We talked nonstop about life since we each left town, classmates, adventures we had been on, and our school and work lives.

I was astonished when I glanced up to see it was 11:00 p.m. Reluctantly, we took our leave.

We had to go back to Smitty's to pick my car up. Brian slid into the driver's seat of his Subaru, the dash throwing bluish light across his cheekbones and forehead. He looked over at me and smiled, his eyes warm in the cool light. "Hey," he said softly, "I really enjoyed this tonight. I haven't had a date since I broke up with Liane last year." He had told me about that, how his long-term relationship had dissolved under the pressures of long distance when Lianne took a job in Florida.

I smiled back. "Me too. This summer hasn't exactly been the easiest one I've had."

He nodded, then reached out to take my hand. "I know."

I felt my heart kick over in my chest.

"I'd like to do this again. Would you?"

"Yes, of course."

We pulled into the lot at Smitty's, Brian wheeling his car around next to mine. He leaned across the seat and brushed his lips gently across mine. "Let's make it soon, okay?"

Chapter Twenty-Five

"So, how was your date last night?" Uncle Jim leaned back in his chair, a grin playing around the corners of his mouth.

I felt myself flush, even though it was coming from him.

"It wasn't a date, okay? We just went for pizza."

I turned away from him so he wouldn't see the corners of my mouth twitching. The memory of that kiss in the car lit up my mind like a meteor.

I hadn't thought about Roger all evening.

"Rachel, is that a smile you're trying to hide from me here?"

The dispatch phone trilled, saving me from answering.

In the glass dispatcher's cubicle, I saw Diane turn her head to make eye contact with me.

"Uh oh...looks like you're getting this one." Uncle Jim said.

Diane ended the call and rolled her chair back so she could stick her head out the door.

"Hey, Rachel. This one's yours. A bat in the house, 157 Sycamore Street."

I pushed my chair back and rose to my feet. Uncle Jim leaned back in his chair, rubbing his chin thoughtfully.

I thought a moment, then asked, "Hey Diane...is that the Lady's home?"

The "Lady's Home" was a brick three story Victorian that housed a half dozen widows. Started in the late 1980s, the informal 'home' was frequented by a changing collection of aging single women. They had banded together to rent rooms in the graceful old home to save money and have company as they navigated the so-called "Golden Years."

"Yup." Diane called out. "Better beat feet over there: that was Lily Harris calling it in, and she sounded dang near hysterical."

I groaned as Uncle Jim chuckled.

"Hey kiddo, it's a rite of passage in this town. I had the bat calls last year."

"Why didn't Joe do them?" I pushed my chair back and rose to my feet, shoving the radio onto my belt.

"He never answered his pager when it was one of those."

I stopped and looked at him. "Why?"

Uncle Jim shrugged. "I dunno. You'd have to ask him." A smile lurked at the edge of his mouth. I eyed him suspiciously. He opened his brilliant blue eyes wide in mock innocence.

"Go. They're waiting for you!"

I muttered under my breath as I left the room. But even a bat call couldn't kill the high I still had from the night before. I was smiling as I yanked the door of the Paddy Waggin' open in a screech, releasing musty dog smells.

Nothing was going to kill my buzz today.

The "Lady's Home" was located on a large corner lot at the intersection of Sycamore and Alice Street. I looked up at the graceful sweep of its mansard roof and circular tower, noting the mullion paned windows and peeps of stained glass around the front door. The white paint around the windows was peeling in places and ivy climbed the north wall, but it was neat and well kept up. A front porch had an empty glider swing, and a walker parked by the door. I grabbed a net out of the back and trudged up the granite pathway, my mind still replaying last night. A bronze lion head door knocker spotted with age greeted me. Smiling, I grasped the ring in its mouth and rapped sharply.

Silence, then I heard a scream, faint, echoey...and terrified.

"Jesus!" My heart rate ratcheted. I peered through the window to the side of the door. Another scream sounded, this one joined by a second voice.

I grabbed the doorknob, hesitated, my mind momentarily going blank. Could I go in or not? My conversation with Timmy Butler at Prudence's about exigent circumstances ran through my mind.

I turned the knob and pulled the door open.

A graceful staircase of polished wood swept down from the second floor, spilling out into an arc of shining wooden floor in front of me. To my right was a parlor in pink and green with upholstered chairs and a fireplace. To my left was a dining room, with a table capable of seating twelve under a darkened but still glittering glass chandelier. Both were empty.

I heard the screams again, coming from the back of the house.

"Miz Harris? Are you okay? It's Rachel from the Brownville Police, here about the bat."

"Get in here now!" Another shriek rang out, joined by others.

"Geeze Louise...what in tarnation is going on in there?" I chose the right side room and advanced into the house. The screams rang out again, louder and from many throats.

The back door of the parlor was a swinging door that opened into the kitchen. Gripping my net firmly, I peered into the room...and stopped short at the sight.

The kitchen was massive, with a commercial size stove along the back and a large prep table in front of it. To the left it ran into what looked like a utility room, with laundry machines, racks for clothing to hang and dry on, and tables for folding things.

A small brown bat darted from side to side in terror, seeking a way out. Screams rang out from every corner.

Under the prep tables and around the room, eight women crouched, each one clutching a laundry basket over her head. More baskets were strewn around the room, flung in panic. Laundry was spread in drifts across the floor, underpants, shirts and unmentionables.

The bat swooped across the room, banking sharply and diving down until it barely cleared two women clutching plastic baskets over their heads. Their shrieks split my ears.

From under the table, Lily Harris lifted the green basket off her head enough to make eye contact with me.

"Don't just stand there! DO SOMETHING!"

The bat whisked by my face, a wind draft brushing my eyes at his passing.

I stood stock still, processing the sight. All I could think of was, why did they have so many laundry baskets?

"Get it before it gets in my hair and lays eggs!" The shriek came from under a white laundry basket in the far corner of the room. Brown stocking clad legs scrabbled for purchase on the shiny linoleum floor as the rather large woman they were attached to attempted to pull herself entirely under the basket. I looked at her closer.

"Mrs. Winslow? Is that you?"

The basket raised up over her face a few inches, revealing the pale gray eyes of my former sixth-grade teacher.

"Eh? Who is it? My eyes aren't what they used to be."

"It's me, Rachel, Rachel Tillison. Gosh, it's been a few years. How have you been Mrs. Winslow?"

The bat fluttered in front of the big mullion paned window over the sink. From under the prep table, Lily Harris shouted, "For the love of God, girl! Stop the talking and get that thing out of here before it gets tangled in someone's hair!"

I sighed in exasperation. "Look, calm down ladies. It won't get tangled in your hair and they don't lay eggs; they're mammals. It's just a flying mouse."

A chorus of shrieks greeted that calming statement. Lily raised the basket higher, fixing me with a sharp glare. "Somehow THAT isn't making any of us feel better, young lady! Now, would you please get that thing out of here?"

I rolled my eyes and brandished my net. "Okay. Hang on; he's out of here in a jiffy."

The bat had been flying back and forth across the kitchen as we talked. As I shook my net out, it sensed it and made a panicked loop around the room. I spun, trying to keep an eye on it. He banked off the wall in the rear of the kitchen and made a sharp left turn.

Right at my face.

I swiped the net at him, which he adeptly avoided with a little juke to the right and down...straight into the top of my head. I felt wings fluttering and banging on my skull as his feet drove deep into my hair...effectively tangling him right on the top of my head.

Now I know about bats. I grew up with them. We used to watch them in the summer lying on our backs in the yard. I caught more than one in my house growing up. Never had I ever been afraid of one.

Until now.

The feel of scrambling feet and panicked wings on my head sent me stumbling forward, swiping blindly at my scalp. Around me, the ladies shrieked in unison. I could hear one voice shouting out, "See? See? We warned you, Miss Smarty Pants!"

It sounded like Mrs. Winslow.

I plunged across the kitchen blindly and into the wall. I felt the doorknob under my back and grabbed it. The door opened, spilling me out onto the pocket sized back porch. Two strides and I was airborne, launching like a yard dart down the steps into the backyard. The bat freed himself as I fell and rocketed away, ripping strands of hair off my head as he did so.

I hit the grass face first, seeing stars as I landed.

I lay there panting, feeling the world revolve slowly around me. Behind me, I heard tentative footsteps on the porch.

"Rachel? Rachel? He's gone. You can get up now." Mrs. Winslow called to me.

Behind her, I heard shuffling steps. Rolling over, I raised my head to see Lily Harris glaring down at me.

"I told you they get in your hair and lay eggs! You smarty-pants college kids always think you know everything!"

I closed my eyes and flopped my head back down.

My buzz was gone.

Chapter Twenty-Six

"Brownville ACO, over."

I reached down and grabbed the mic while keeping my eyes on the bumpy, rutted dirt road I was navigating down. To my right, the Sawmill River bumped and burbled along. On my left, Morton's Farm lazed under the sun, the rolling fields dotted with black and white heifers.

I was on a mission.

"Brownville ACO copy." I recognized Diane's voice on the other end.

"Hey Rachel, we have a complaint of a cat in a tree at 17 Merry Lane. The caller thinks it's Ruth Johnson's cat."

I suppressed the groan that threatened.

"Cats in trees? Since when do I have to climb trees?"

"Since now. The caller was Mrs. Santos."

The chief's wife. And friend of Ruth Johnson's.

I sighed deeply. "Roger that, Diane. I'm over on Spittle Creek Road now. I'll head that way."

Well, so much for my mission of investigating Prudence Coolidge's neighbor. I looked for a place to turn the Paddy Waggin' around. The river curved away from the roadway here, and trees now lined the right side of the van. I caught a flash of metal in the leaves on the right: a dirt driveway angled off into the woods; the metal was an ominous sign:

'Do not turn around here! Danger! Trespassers will be persecuted to the full extent of the law! Do not enter!'

The sign tilted to the right; the paint flaking and faded. Bullet holes peppered it where someone had used it as a target. The driveway led up into the land owned by Buck Checker, Mrs. Coolidge's oddball neighbor, the very same person I was on my way to find.

I nosed the Paddy Waggin' into the drive and hesitated a moment. Merry Lane was a good fifteen minutes away, and I was already out here. A few more minutes wouldn't make that big a difference, now would it? It wasn't like you ever saw cat skeletons in trees, anyway.

The mystery dog napper went through my mind. What the hell: I was already here. Ignoring the sign, I goosed the throttle and eased the Paddy Waggin' over the hump in the driveway and headed into the woods.

It was pretty obvious Buck Checker didn't like visitors. Another sign hung some twenty feet in, this one warning that he would shoot first and ask questions later. I thought about Buck and what I knew about him. He had always been a bit weird, a recluse hunter mountain man type who kept to himself. I could still see him coming into town when I was a little girl, his hair red and unruly under his stained Carhartt cap, often in a ponytail that hung to his waist. His face was usually buried in an equally unruly red beard. Glasses filled the space between beard and cap. Wild brown eyes peered out at the world, ready for the next attack.

I also remembered his gentleness in speaking to me, when, as a ten-year-old, I had cowered away from him. We had been in the Five and Dime, where I was poking about the displays impatiently waiting for my mother. He had looked at Mrs. Cook, who guarded the candy counter from the likes of me and asked her to let me pick out a hard candy. He had dropped the coin on the counter and winked at me before leaving.

I was confident he wasn't the threat he was making himself out to be. And I really wanted to know why someone who looked an awful lot like him had been seen on the Mannion's security video letting Suzy out of her fenced-in yard.

The Paddy Waggin' shuddered and groaned as I scraped over a large boulder that stuck up out of the driveway, a rather magnanimous name for the rutted track Buck lived on. It took another few minutes before I rounded the last turn to Buck's abode. And that was also a magnanimous name for it.

Once it was a gleaming doublewide with a square and true roof and wide glass windows. Now it was a sagging memory of happier times. Saplings poked up around the foundation, a loose name for the plywood that covered the base of the trailer. The once cheery yellow had faded down the color wheel to a dingy mustard tan. A lazy curl of smoke twined out of the stovepipe and Buck's old Chevy truck was parked in the dirt patch next to it. The forest crowded around the clearing, dense shade even at the height of the day. A rutted path snaked away from the driveway and meandered up the slope, deeper into the woods. I could just see the faded wooden walls and tilted smokestack of an old sugar shack. Behind the home, a small stream burbled over moss-covered boulders at the edge of the woods.

I felt a chill crawl down my spine. I eyed the area with increasing misgivings. My memory of him from that day was almost 13 years old now. I glanced around to see if I could discreetly back away from the trailer and turn around.

Movement caught my eye. The door opened about halfway, revealing a dark square. A rifle barrel slid through the opening the business end aimed directly at me. I felt my eyes bug out of my head. I fumbled at the door and rolled the window down.

"Hey! Buck? It's me: Rachel Tillison! I'm no threat to you!" My voice squeaked at the end.

The barrel stayed steady on me. A crazy brown eye peered around the doorjamb above it.

"What do ya want? Yer trespassin'! Dinja read dem signs, girl?"

"Yes sir Mr. Checker, I did. I wanted to talk to you for a minute about some stuff that's going on around here, see if you can help me."

Beads of sweat trickled down my temples.

. . .

He poked his head out further, fixing me with a baleful look. I noticed his hair, once fire engine red, was now snowy white. It still hung to his waist, caught up in a snarled ponytail. "Who the heck are you, girl? I don't know you."

"We've met before, sir. My dad is Marty Tillison. We have the farm over to the river side of town, The Three Belles Farm."

The barrel lowered slightly. "Eh? Marty's girl, you say?"

"Yes sir. I am."

"Well, whatta ya doing in this contraption, then?" He gestured at the Paddy Waggin's with the muzzle of the rifle.

"I'm the Animal Control Officer in town now, sir. I'm trying to find some lost dogs, and I was hoping you'd seen something."

The barrel crept back up to bear on me. "I ain't seen no dogs! Now git on outta here!"

"Okay, okay. I won't stay. Just one more question, though: have you seen any large white animals around here?"

The door screeched as he shoved it fully open, stepping onto the narrow porch. He was thin to the point of being emaciated, his pants sagging around nonexistent hips.

"A white animal? You saw a white animal? Where? Where'd you see it?"

I tilted my head at the urgency in his voice.

"I saw it over to the train crossing and Prudence Coolidge said it tried to attack her."

"When? When did that happen?"

"Ye-yesterday?" I didn't like the crazed look he had, nor the way he was aiming at me more carefully now.

He swore. "Gol-dang-it-all!"

"What is it Mr. Checker?"

"Git! Git offa my land, girl, go on! Go now before I fill you with lead shot!"

"But Mr. Checker..."

The muzzle flashed, the crack of the rifle booming in my ears. Leaves and chunks of bark rained down on the van.

"Git or the next one's got your name on it!"

I slammed the Paddy Waggin in reverse and began heading backwards as fast as I could.

Over the screeching and thumping of the rocks on the underside of the van, I thought I could hear dogs barking.

Chapter Twenty-Seven

"A large white animal, you say? What the heck could it be?" Sandy Case, Uncle Jim's girlfriend and news reporter, was perched on the edge of the filing cabinet in the office on this sunny afternoon, a pad of paper in her hand. She chewed on her lower lip in concentration.

"I've seen it myself; it's huge. And Prudence said it tried to attack her, said it was making weird noises and ran at her."

"So what do you think it is, then?" Sandy tapped her front tooth with the pen. Uncle Jim watched her, a whipped expression on his face. I hid a smile; Uncle Jim didn't have a good poker face.

I shrugged. "I never got that good a look. I thought it was a steer: it left hoof prints like an ox or something. But Addison's are adamant it's not theirs and Prudence is of the mind that it was trying to attack her. Said it ran after her bellowing."

Sandy flipped a page in her notebook. "And she said it had big horns and stood 7 feet tall. What around here is like that?"

Jim shrugged his shoulder. "Beats me. Unless it's some mutant ox, the average steer stands a lot smaller than that."

Sandy pinned him with her eyes, making Uncle Jim flush. "What about non-domestic animals? What else could it be?"

Jim shrugged. "Ah cain't rightly say.

Sandy slid off the filing cabinet. "Yeah, well, if there's one thing I've learned the past year here is anything is possible. Rachel, you have anything to say about it?"

"Now hold on there, Sandy. You cain't be interviewing Rachel about it!"

"Well, why not? She's the animal control officer."

"And she's my niece, too. Come on Sandy; Ah swear you just are a cantankerous woman at times."

She shoved her notebook in the voluminous bag she always carried, pinning him with a stare. "And that is exactly why you like me." She pecked him on the cheek, sending a red flush up his face.

"Rachel, if you decide to chat, call me." She swept out of the room, leaving a light floral scent behind her.

I struggled to hide the smile that was threatening. Behind the scarred wooden desk, Uncle Jim fidgeted, his face flaming. A chuckle snuck out of me.

"You just shut your mouth, Rachel."

I gave up trying to hold it in and laughed out loud. "I

swear, I have never seen you so tongue tied around a woman before!"

Uncle Jim shook his head. "She ain't no ordinary woman, that's for sure!"

I smiled at that. "No, she certainly isn't. But you know... maybe it wouldn't be a bad thing to get her help with investigating these dognappings. She knows how to find stuff."

"I dunno, Rach. Sandy's dang good at that kinda stuff, but she's actually afraid of dogs."

I arched an eyebrow at him. "Say what? Sandy? Afraid?"

He pushed himself back from his desk and nodded. "Ah do believe she is. She makes a fuss about dogs, complains about their poop, the noise, all that. But deep down, Ah believe she's plain old, afraid of 'em."

"Huh. Well, I never woulda thought that. I mean, like, Sandy? Scared of anything? After last year?"

Uncle Jim's girlfriend had made one hell of an impression on Brownville when she ended up smack in the middle of the first murder this town had seen in, like, forever. The fallout had shaken the town to the core, especially the police department.

She sure shook things up, both in Brownville and in my family.

"So, we need to talk about your run in with Buck Checker yesterday." Uncle Jim broke into my reverie.

"I told you everything about it; I don't know what else we need to discuss." I was still smarting from the tongue lashings I had received both from Uncle Jim and from Mom.

"Girl, you cain't go doing stuff like that. And now we got ourselves a pickle. Buck was within his right to order you off his land, but shooting over your head adds a new spin to it. He ain't someone you want to get into a fight with, but we also don't want him thinking he can get away with murder, either."

I grimaced at his choice of words.

"Uncle Jim..." I paused, momentarily unsure of myself. "I didn't get a chance to tell you this yesterday, being that you were pretty ticked at the time, but I coulda sworn I heard a whole bunch of dogs barking when I was beating feet outta there."

He tilted his chair back and placed a foot on the lower drawer. "Well, he's usually got a whole buncha Walker Hounds hanging around. Buck and some of his friends like to hunt."

"I know. I've seen his dogs before. But...these didn't sound like hounds. I mean, there was a lot of noise going on, and I was kinda freaked out, but I swear at least some of them sounded yappy."

Uncle Jim swore softly. "Now you tell me that."

"Well, you were sorta angry yesterday..."

He snorted. " Sorta. Sorta. Yeah, I was 'sorta' angry alright. Not the least of which was because we had to send Damion to the cat call! If the Chief ever found out what you were up to, he'd have blown a gasket!"

Damion Fellows was one of the gangly reserve officers our department had. About all of 19, he was the last of the last resorts. He was a nice kid, a sweet one actually, but he was also pretty gullible, something that worked against you at times.

He also had developed a distinct crush on me, something I was partly exasperated and partly amused by.

I tried to sound chastened. "I know. Sorry."

Uncle Jim fixed me with a stare. "Keep it up and I'm gonna send you out to do barn inspections next."

I rolled my eyes. "You know; you haven't really talked to me anymore about what they are going to do with me here. I thought you were going to talk to the Chief about expanding my job, letting me do some IT stuff. I have a degree in that, not dog catching."

Uncle Jim started pushing papers around on his desk, avoiding my stare. "I'll talk to him. The time hasn't been right."

"Why not?"

"Well, for one thing, you keep getting yourself in a pickle, young lady! If'n you could stop having people shooting at you or burning buildings down, maybe we can get someplace with it."

Geeze. These folks were awfully picky about how I did my job sometimes.

"Fine." I stood up and shoved my chair back under the desk. Uncle Jim looked up from his papers at me. "I'm booking off for the day. Damion can get any calls until tomorrow."

"Go." He gestured toward the door. "And go do something fun, act like a college kid. You need it."

As I walked down the hallway, I pondered that last statement. I hadn't felt like a real 'college kid' since arriving here.

Chapter Twenty-Eight

"Brownville ACO, over."

I reached for the radio on the dash of the Paddy Waggin'. Why did these calls always come in at 4:45 on a Friday afternoon?

"Brownville ACO here. What's up?"

I heard Diane on the other end. "Yeah Rachel, you have a call just came in. Caller reporting a loose piglet over on Bollinger Street. Said it's at the end of the street near the pond."

I sighed. "A pig? I have to chase pigs now too?"

"Anything with fur, feathers, or four legs is yours. Doesn't sound very big. Might belong to Bobby Beleeno. I heard he went up to the auction last week and came home with a bunch of things."

"Great. Well, as long as it isn't another one of those emus, it's ok with me. Brownville ACO en route."

The sun was sending long slanting rays through the maple trees as I cruised down Bollinger, searching for the errant piglet. Victorian homes gave way to Colonial style, then to 1970s raised ranch houses. The manicured lawns slowly became larger and shaggier, speckled with kids' toys and chicken coops.

I cast my gaze from side to side as I cruised, searching for the errant piglet. Where a strip of woods met the road, I spied movement. Rooting merrily away under the roots of a massive oak tree, his curled tail wagging, was the piglet.

I was relieved to see it was small, small enough to pick up and put in a dog crate.

Pulling over, I parked the van and grabbed my net out of the back.

The piglet paused his rooting and eyed me warily when I stepped out.

"Hey piggy, piggy, piggy. Whatchu doin'?" I called to him.

He gave me a side eye and resumed his rooting, little grunts filling the air.

I sidled around behind him, working my way closer.

"Come here, little buddy."

Bright brown eyes appraised me as he paused his rooting again. I inched a little bit closer.

I stood still and waited a moment. Deciding I was no threat, he started rooting and digging, shoving his hard, flat nose into the mound of dead leaves and acorns at the base of the tree.

It was the moment I was waiting for.

The net whooshed as I swung it down over him, a clean catch. With a shriek, he launched into the netting and began to squeal like he was being murdered.

I pounced on him, bracketing the screaming piglet in the net with my knees, my ears ringing from his squeals.

Holy cow, the little guy had a set of lungs on him.

"Come on, little man. No one's going to hurt you. Let's get you in a crate and back home, where you belong."

I had picked him up while tangled in the netting. Grasping his hind legs, I let him hang upside down momentarily while I freed him. His screams were bloodcurdling.

"Geez Louise! No one is killing you, okay?"

I rose from the ground, holding the piglet by the hind legs with both hands. I turned to take him to the van...and found Buster between me and the Paddy Waggin'. Every hair on his spine was standing straight up. I couldn't hear him over the piglet, but I could see the movement of his head as he "chuffed" at me.

Oh, no...not again.

The piglet shrieked deafeningly.

Buster's slit pupiled eyes were fixed on me. Menace dripped from every pore on him.

I guess he was still holding a grudge from the last time.

"Oh, come on Buster. Give it a break. No one is doing anything to you." Slowly, I edged sideways toward the open side door of the van. I was hoping to leap inside before he could reach me.

He turned, keeping his eyes fixed on me, and stomped a front foot. I stopped. The piglet screamed at a new level and Buster tensed, stomping a foot again.

Slowly, I lowered the piglet to the ground, releasing his rear legs. With one last squeal, he bolted away. Buster momentarily turned his head as he fled and I made a break for it.

Dirt flew from underfoot as I sprinted around him for the van. But Buster hadn't been on his own all these years without learning to be wily. With a "chuff," he lowered his head and charged after me.

I couldn't turn to the right hard enough at the speed I was going to make it into the open door, so I sprinted around the back of the van. I figured Buster would follow.

I was wrong.

As I cleared the nose of the van, he confronted me, waiting right at the side door for me.

Darn, this damn goat was smart! I reversed direction. This time he took chase, head down, charging after my heels, inches behind. I cleared the back of the van at a run, the open door scant feet away, and that was when the piglet took his revenge.

He must have ended up under the Paddy Waggin' because suddenly he was running out from underneath it, right into my path. I caught his roly- poly little body with my left foot and was instantly airborne.

Leaves flew as I crashed face first onto the ground, the piglets squealing ringing in my ears. I heard a loud "chuff" from behind me, and instinctively covered my head.

Buster the Devil Goat landed squarely on the small of my back, then reared up, driving his horns down smack between my shoulder blades.

The air left my lungs and I swear my soul did too.

I gasped for air that was nonexistent as his black cloven feet appeared at the edge of my vision.

"Oh, crap!" I thought, being that I was unable to say it.

I guess he was satisfied with his work because I heard rustling and the feet went away.

Slowly molecules of air began to make it into my lungs again.

I heard rustling again. Cringing, I squeezed my eyes shut, hoping if I played dead, he would leave me alone.

Warm acorn scented air puffed on my face.

I opened one eye a slit to see a wet hard nose inches from my face, snuffling in my aroma. Curious brown eyes peered down at me, eyes that were oddly human seen from this close.

Opening my eyes further, I found we were alone.

The piglet snorted and spooked away as I rolled back onto my knees. I gasped in a lungful of air, feeling the throbbing in my upper and lower back.

Holy hell. This was it. I was not going to deal with Buster any longer. Someone must have owned him at one time. If it was the last thing I did, I was going to catch that devil goat and get him back to them.

Maybe they would make curried goat out of him.

Chapter Twenty-Nine

Monday dawned bright and cheery across the verdant river valley. I squinted against the glare, my head banging from lack of sleep, a lack thanks to Buster's assault on my back. The lack of sleep and lack of coffee was working against me as I trundled across the narrow roads that criss-crossed the 'Meadows' section of Brownville. I glanced at the address on the paper again; Meredith Malloy at 38 Searles Cross Road, complaining about missing some of her chickens.

I didn't know her; she was one of the recent transplants to Brownville, by all accounts lured here after the news about last year's murder and investigation. A sleepy little town like this never found itself front and center like that. The result was an influx of people who were attracted to the idea of a utopia along the river banks.

It was a mixed blessing for us.

38 Searles Cross Road was a cute little house with east-facing windows that twinkled in the light, sending a stab of pain through my temple. Brown sided with dark red shutters, it was a two story doll house with a fenced front garden

and a larger back yard. I could see a large chicken coop with wire fenced run dominating the area. About thirty or more hens and a couple of roosters kicked and scratched outside the coop.

I glanced up, wondering if the missing chickens would be as simple as a red-tailed hawk in the area.

The door opened as I pulled into the small driveway and Meredith emerged onto the stoop, wringing her hands in worry. Round glasses framed watery blue eyes. Her hair was gray streaked, brushing her shoulders. Dirty jeans and a flannel shirt crowned with a pair of pink Crocs completed her look.

I suppressed a sigh as I crawled out of the Paddy Waggin'. "Morning Ms. Malloy. I'm Rachel Tillison, Brownville Animal Control Officer. What's going on here today, ma'am?"

Her hands wrung and twitched. "I'm so glad you are here. I came out this morning and Patty was missing. Rhonda is going to be so upset!"

I pulled my notebook out. "And Patty is a what?"

"She's a Buff Orpington, one of the finest!

"Yes, ma'am." I scratched down a couple of words. "And who is Rhonda?"

"Rhonda is her best friend. If Patty is gone, then Alex is going to be so angry!"

"I assume Rhonda is a chicken also, ma'am?"

"Of course she is! She's that barred rock over there!" She gestured toward the birds pecking at the grass.

"Mmm-hmm. When did you last see, uh, Patty?"

"John was here and Patty came running over to see him. I thought he was acting strange, but I chalked it up to the weather. When he left, Patty was gone too!"

"I see. And who is John, ma'am?"

"John is a Brahma that lives a few houses up the road. He comes down here all the time. Oh, Alex is going to be so angry!"

"I assume Alex is also a chicken?"

"Of course not! Alex Decarlo; he's the man who sold me my birds when I moved here. He told me I had to take special care of Patty, that Esther would be heartbroken if anything happened to her."

I knew Alex Decarlo. An odd man, he was passionate about his birds.

"Could a predator have eaten her?"

"Lucy would never allow that!"

"Who is Lucy, ma'am?"

"Lucy is my Llama."

My head was starting to ache.

"Okay." I scratched a couple more notes. "Who is Esther?"

"Esther is a silkie hen."

"So, let me recap this then. Patty is missing. Rhonda is upset. John came to visit and Patty disappeared. Alex is going to be angry. Esther is going to be heartbroken. Lucy wouldn't let her be eaten. Is that correct?"

"I didn't get to tell you about Michael yet."

"Who is Michael?"

She turned and gestured toward a red and green rooster who was strutting back and forth, fixing a baleful eye on me.

"That's Michael. And Michael came from Mary. I think Mary is jealous of me. I think Mary stole Patty."

Oh, dear God.

"So who is Mary?"

"Mary is a Laced Wyandotte that comes here with John sometimes. Mary is terribly jealous of me."

"Ma'am...you think a...hen...is jealous of you?"

"Well, of course! Chickens are very particular, you know."

"How can one chicken steal another one?" My head began to slowly throb.

"Don't underestimate the power of poultry, young lady! Chickens are very smart, particularly when they are in a flock. The get a hive mentality."

"Wouldn't that be a coop mentality, then?"

"Are you mocking me?"

"No ma'am. I would never do that."

She sniffed, wiped her nose with the back of her hand. "There're dirty doings here, I tell you, dirty doings."

"Ms. Malloy, you have one hen missing. It's distressing, but it probably isn't dirty doings."

"But it's Patty who is missing! Of all the hens, she is the least likely to do that."

"To do what? Get eaten by something?" As soon as I said it, I knew it was the wrong thing to say.

"Oh!" She buried her face in her hands. "Don't even say such a thing! Randall would never stand for this, never!"

"Randall?" I stared at her, my pen hovering above the pad. "Who is Randall? Another chicken?"

"Of course not! Don't be silly! Randall is my husband."

"So, um, okay, when did you last see, uh, Patty?" I looked at my notes in consternation; the names scribbled in writing that resembled chicken scratch.

"I saw her yesterday afternoon, after we got done playing dress up with everyone."

I looked up at her. I could feel my right eye twitching.

"Dress up? I'm sorry, I don't follow you, ma'am?" Did she mean dressing out her birds?

"Dress up! You know, when you dress them for special

occasions. It was Penelope's second hatch day, so we cele-brated with dressing everyone up."

"How...how do you dress a chicken?" As soon as the words left my mouth, I regretted it.

Her face lit up. "Oh! It's so much fun! Here, wait a minute!" She hopped off the stoop and skipped across the yard to the shed attached to the coop.

"Uh, ma'am? Ma'am?"

She waved a hand dismissively at me and disappeared into the shed. She popped out, clutching brightly colored fabric in her hand. A massive Brahma hen pecked at the dirt around her feet: she snatched it up off the ground and began stretching the fabric over its head.

I watched in horrified fascination.

"Here you go!" She held the hen up, now resplendent in a colorful skirt and a cap that had dreadlocks hanging down on either side of the beady eyed bird. "This is 'Brahma Mama'!"

I was staring at her with the rapt attention one gives to a car wreck; you know you shouldn't stare, but you can't look away.

"And look at this one..." She plopped "Brahma Mama" on the ground and disappeared back into the shed. Popping back out, she grabbed a nearby Golden Comet hen up and started tugging fabric over her chest.

"Ta dah!" She held up the hen, who now sported a tiny black jacket and a silver helmet, "This is 'Biker Chick'!"

Oh, dear God.

"And look at this..." She spun to hop back into the shed. I couldn't take another one.

"Ma'am, please, we have to have an investigation here. That's all very nice, but it isn't going to help get," I paused to look at my notes, "Patty back."

She pressed her two fists to her mouth. Tears glittered. "Someone must have taken her. Patty would never wander off. She loves me!"

"Ma'am, this is Brownville. No one would take your bird. We don't do things like that here."

"Then you need to find her pronto! Suppose she's out there somewhere, lost and frightened? Maybe she's hurt. Maybe she fell down into a well!" The tears that had threatened spilled over into a waterfall.

Oh, brother. Dressed up birds were definitely the lesser of two evils here.

"You were about to show me another costume?"

Chapter Thirty

"There you are. Where have you been? I was about to send Rusty out to look for you." Uncle Jim swiveled his chair around to face me as I stomped into the room.

"Ugh, I like had to spend hours over at Mrs. Malloy's house. Did you know she dresses her chickens in little costumes?"

He chuckled, "Boy Rach, you certainly attract 'em, don't you?"

I tossed my keys down on the desk, the metallic rattle sending spears of pain through my eyes. Uncle Jim eyed me for a moment.

"What's up with you?"

I shook my head. "Nothin'."

"Huh. Somehow that doesn't look like 'nothin' to me."

"I'm fine. I have a headache, is all." My head throbbed in time to my heartbeat.

Uncle Jim sighed and gestured toward the computer. "Just a heads up; that hurricane off the coast of South Carolina, Hurricane Greta, is changing course. The weather nerds are saying it's going to come straight up the coast and right up through Connecticut and hit us square."

I snorted. "A hurricane? Here? Yeah, whoopee, that means a day of rain is all."

Uncle Jim shook his head. "Don't discount it Rach. We had that one in 2011, Hurricane Irene. About wiped some places right off the map."

Walking around my desk, I pulled the chair out and sat down. "I was like ten when that happened. I remember the road being closed for days and no school. Even so, that was a fluke. We're one hundred and fifty miles from the coast, Uncle Jim. I seriously doubt it's going to be anything."

"Maybe not, but if'n it does, we have to open the shelter at the school. And that includes one for pets. And that's gonna be your responsibility. So you may want to find the cages and crates we have in the sheds out back in case you need 'em in a hurry."

I sighed and rubbed my eyes. "When is this one predicted to arrive here, then?"

Uncle Jim scrolled down the computer page, frowning as he read it. "They're talking sometime Wednesday afternoon."

"Where are the shed keys?"

Uncle Jim opened a drawer on his desk and rifled around. "Here. It's the one on the yellow fob." He tossed it into the out basket on his desk.

"So have you spoken to the Captain yet about my job? I keep hearing about more and more things I am supposed to do, but I haven't heard of any additional pay or benefits yet. Mom's on my case pretty hard about it."

Uncle Jim looked away and mumbled, "Yeah, I tried to talk to him last week, and he was pretty busy. I am planning on talking to him soon."

My head throbbed dully. "Uncle Jim, I really need to know sooner than later here. If I can't get more money and insurance, I am going to have to start job hunting again. I especially can't keep having Buster beat me up like this without insurance."

Roger flashed through my skull, causing a massive thump. His face was followed quickly by Brian's. Dang it all; why did everything have to be so complicated all the time?

Chapter Thirty-One

Amanda was waiting for me at the seats outside of the Brownville Market, two steaming cups of tea and scones waiting. I smiled when I caught a glimpse of her, her blonde hair in wisps around her face. I really was lucky to have her as my friend.

We had met in kindergarten, the first day, actually. I had felt like she was my sister then and now, some 16 years later; I felt the same.

"Hey you!" I tugged the wrought-iron chair out and plunked down across from her.

"And hey yourself, Missy." Her eyes twinkled at me as she gingerly took a sip of her tea.

I sighed, feeling the knot of tension starting to ease as I looked around me. Traffic crept up Main Street, halting as people jay walked across to the market. Across the street I saw a tall beanpole of a man, a ragged trench coat flapping around his knees. A slender woman walked in his shadow, her demeanor cautious. One Eyed Joe and April, two of the residents down by the river. Last year, Sandy got to know some of them pretty well when she almost drowned. I had never really given the homeless residents much of a thought before that. But we surely paid attention now. Uncle Jim was down there weekly, it seemed, dropping off food or clothing for them, just making sure they were okay. He was going to look out for them forever now. We all were.

"So, how's the new job going?" I asked as I blew on my tea.

"Ugh, I hate starting a new job," she sighed and blew a strand of hair out of her face. "Yesterday we had this absolute wanker come in, a real piece of work."

"Yeah? Who?"

She shrugged, "Dunno. An out of towner. I've never seen him before and hope to never see him again."

Amanda had just started at the Crusty Tart, a new bake shop in town. I had been eyeing it when I drove through town lately. I took a bite of my scone, crumbs trickling down my chin.

"This guy marches in, acting like he is King Philip or something. Just pushed his way up to the counter and demanded I wait on him first. Looked like a real city fop, right down to the cuffed pants. Anyway, Donnie Lewis was there, was next in line actually. It didn't go so good."

Donnie Lewis was a couple of years ahead of us in school. He was a big guy, now an auto mechanic over at the shop on Route 7. He didn't say much; he didn't have to. I felt a grin threatening at the thought of some wanker pushing his way in front of Donnie.

"So, um, did Donnie, like, show him out?"

Amanda snorted. "It would have been easier on that dude if he had. No, Donnie taught him a lesson on patience."

I cocked my head at her. A smile crept across her face.

"Come on; spill it. What happened?"

"Um. He might have, like, locked him in the men's room for a while?" The grin broke out in full force.

I laughed out loud. "Oh my God, no he didn't!"

She nodded. "Oh yes, he did! Marched him in and shoved a chair under the knob. Wouldn't let him out until he and the other two people waiting were done. Boy, that dude was pissed! He was yelling about dumb locals and how we were all gonna regret treating him like that, blah blah. He never did order anything."

I snorted into my hand. "Oh man, was Bruce there?" Bruce was the owner.

"No, thank God, because I wouldn't want to see Donnie and Bruce lock horns. No, Bruce came in later and just kinda said, well I can't control all my customers now, can I?" Bruce's way of agreeing with Donnie.

"Never a dull moment around here, is there?" I sipped my now cooling tea. Across the street I could see April and One Eyed Joe still. They had sat down on one of the benches along the street. As I looked across Main Street at them, I saw a short man dressed in a suit striding along the sidewalk. His thinning hair rose off of his narrow forehead, rimless glasses perched on his nose. He carried a brown leather briefcase in his left hand; his right clutched a cell phone to his ear. I caught him scowling at Joe and April.

Joe caught it too. I saw his mouth move as he said something to the man.

Now One Eyed Joe was an interesting man. A car accident years ago left him with some sort of condition that made him talk funny. Sometimes he spoke in intelligible sentences. Other times, he spoke backwards. That same accident made him lose his eye too, leaving the other one looking large in his narrow face. If you didn't know him, you would brush him off. That was a mistake. He wasn't dumb. And he saw everything that happened around town.

Whatever that man said, it made April shrink down and Joe stand up, looking down on the shorter man. Joe's mouth moved again, and the man flushed red. He sidled around Joe and hurried away, his suit coat flapping in the breeze he made. Obviously, Joe was having a good moment where he was understandable.

Amanda looked around to see what I was staring at. "Hey! That's the guy!" She pointed at the man as he double timed his way up Main Street.

"Really? Well, he just pissed Joe off, too. Joe stood up and said something to him, and that guy skedaddled."

Really, Main Street was better than television sometimes.

"Hey Amanda, can you give me a hand with something?" I watched Joe and April idly as I blew on my steaming cup again.

"Sure. What do you need?" That was one thing I loved about Amanda. She was always there when I needed her. I did the same for her; I'd crawl across broken glass for her, my oldest, best friend.

"Uncle Jim's saying that hurricane is maybe going to turn north. He's thinking we need to get the shelter ready at the high school. I have to get the crates out of the shed and over to the school by Tuesday night."

"Huh. I heard about that, but isn't that a non-issue? I mean, it's not like we are on the coast or anything."

"I know. He's still spooked by Hurricane Irene, I guess."

"Yeah, of course I'll help. When do you want to do it?"

I thought about that a moment. It was Saturday afternoon, the sun high in a cloudless blue bowl of a sky. I had my doubts about going through all the work for nothing. But still, an order was an order.

I sighed. "You have anything going on tomorrow afternoon? Might be best to get in the school when there's no one else there. I have to stash the crates in the equipment storage room for now. Uncle Jim and Rusty will bring the cots over on Tuesday if it looks like they need them."

"Sure. It's a date."

Chapter Thirty-Two

Amanda climbed into her Prius and drove off with one last wave at me. I sighed and tossed my cup into the trash. Despite her calming presence, my nerves still jangled. I couldn't shake Buck Checker, no matter how hard I tried. I kept hearing those dogs over the rattling of the Paddy Waggin' as I hightailed it out of there.

What was going on with him? Why did he get so agitated when I mentioned the white animal? And why did it look like him on camera at Mrs. Homas letting Suzy out?

And why were dogs disappearing in the first place?

I stared across Main Street, not seeing it. The homes the dogs were disappearing from were all in a rough triangle, the center of which was Buck's place.

My unease increased.

I'd never known Buck to be on the wrong side of the law before. Weird, yes. Reclusive, yes. But not unlawful.

Time to take a little closer look.

The Paddy Waggin' was parked on Main Street half a block down. It smelled like a wet dog inside. I grimaced and lowered both front windows, releasing a puff of dog aroma.

As I pulled my seatbelt on, I saw the little man in a suit across the street. He was at Energy Square, the new pocket park Mayor Molly Bruce had dedicated this spring. His briefcase was set on one of the benches, and he had his cell phone clutched to his ear. He was scowling and gesturing broadly at the unseen caller. He looked pissed. I watched him a moment longer, wondering who he was and why he was in Brownville.

I wasn't the only one watching him.

Under the little dogwood tree behind him was another bench, this one inhabited by someone who was reclining under a newspaper tent. As I watched, the paper shifted and fell to the ground, revealing an irritated Willy, one of Joe and April's tribe. His salt and pepper mustache was bristling in indignation.

Unaware of his audience, the man kept yelling into his phone. I could catch snippets from across the street.

Willy was catching a lot more than snippets, though. He reached his saturation point with this dude.

"Oy!" That I heard clear as a bell across the traffic.

The man whirled around. "Oh, for crying out loud! Can't I have any privacy in this crappy town?"

Hey! I felt my hackles rise at that one.

Who WAS this clown?

I fired up the van as the two men squared off nose to nose. Shaking my head, I pulled out into traffic and headed out of town.

I hesitated at the thought of going back to Buck's. His driveway was a one lane narrow path straight into the muzzle of his shotgun. I wasn't too keen to do that again.

But I knew one area I could investigate in relative safety; the woods bordering Thatcher Lane, where Prudence Coolidge lived.

I thought about the geography of the area a bit more. Plain Street meandered along one side of a broad triangle, Bollinger Street made the other side of it. About midway up, Thatcher Lane bisected it. It dead ended about 500 feet from Plain Street, the result of the town closing a bridge over the Sawmill River some decades ago.

Prudence owned the triangle from the intersection of Plain and Bollinger to Thatcher Lane, some 24 acres of overgrown farm land.

The triangle continued to widen from Prudence's place, with Buck Checker's land sharing a property line with her. He had a lot of land, over 100 acres. Combined, the two places covered an impressive swath.

Why the hell would either of them be stealing dogs? It made no sense at all. And Prudence had lost a dog as well, with Luther being among the missing.

And Luther made no sense. All the other dogs were little ones, beloved house pets, leaving behind furious owners. Luther was a hound dog, a tracking dog. He didn't fit the bill.

And what about the mysterious white animal Prudence was so afraid of? Her fear was genuine.

I turned the Paddy Wagon' toward Thatcher Lane.

Chapter Thirty-Three

Thatcher Lane drowsed under the long shadows of the autumn sun. The door to the Paddy Waggin' thumped shut behind me as I crawled out, scanning the roadway back and forth for any signs of people or animals.

The lane was empty.

Tangled bushes lined most of it, giving way grudgingly to the edge of Prudence Collins's land several hundred feet away from where I now stood. After Amos Prill's place had burned down some ten years prior, no one else had built on Thatcher Lane, which dead ended some two hundred feet further up.

Buck's property line began on the north side of Thatcher Lane.

Trying to ignore my misgivings, I grabbed my hiking stick, my cellphone and my backpack and set out toward Buck's place.

Twenty feet into the woods may as well have been two hundred feet in. This side of his land seemed desolate and unused. Saplings gave way to old growth, the ground undulating as I tromped up small hills. At each hilltop, I crouched down and squat-walked to the top, scanning for anyone or anything before continuing.

Periodically, I would stop and check my phone, tracking my progress on the map app. I estimated I had about a quarter of a mile to go before reaching the active area of Buck's land.

A dribble of sweat coursed down my spine as I imagined what would transpire if Buck saw me first. I had no illusions about how he would react.

I had covered about an eighth of a mile when I saw the first disturbance in the soil. An extensive area was churned, freshly dug up. The bark on a larger pine tree showed new, raw scrape marks on it some 8 feet off the churned up ground. Some smaller saplings had been knocked over, the wood gleaming white in the dim light of the undergrowth.

I spotted something in the middle of the area that was out of place, glowing white against the black soil. With a wary look around, I moved into the area and picked it up.

It was a tuft of fur.

It felt coarse against my fingers, not fine like some mammal hair, but rough like the hair on a cow or steer. The hair was about two inches long, a tuft that had been left behind when something had laid down and maybe rolled in this spot. Large flattened spots in the churned dirt painted to a large...and heavy...body having recently reposed there.

I felt a chill snake down my spine. Carefully, I secured the tuft in the front pocket of my backpack.

Turning back to the area, I examined the ground carefully. At the edge of the clearing I saw a distinct set of tracks, cloven hoofed and large, huge actually, heading away in a meandering line.

They were headed toward Buck's house.

I adjusted my backpack and carefully followed the path. Holy Moly, whatever this thing was, it was huge! I stopped and placed my hand inside one especially clear hoof print; it dwarfed my hand. With a nervous glance around, I continued tracking it.

I smelled the wood smoke long before I saw his house. I slowed my pace, now moving from tree to tree as I climbed the last rise above his home. The stovepipe from the old sugar shack peeked up out of the underbrush ahead of me; the shack proper was down the hillside and still hidden. I slowly crept the last ten feet to the top, peeking over the hillside.

From my vantage point, I was about 50 feet behind and slightly above the sugar shack. To my left, the ground sloped down toward the stream. In front of me, it fell to the sugar shack where it leveled out slightly and continued on down to Buck's house. His house was probably a good 75 feet or more away from me here.

The tracks continued down over the hill and disappeared from my sight, hidden by the sugar shack.

Smoke curled gently from the stovepipe on Buck's house; his pickup truck was in the yard.

The area was silent.

I gnawed on my thumbnail as I considered my options. "Rach, you've gone far enough. Don't be a dumbass." I muttered to myself. But still...all this way and I still wasn't close enough. I decided to creep down to the rear of the sugar shack.

The carpet of dead leaves rustled slightly underfoot as I crept down the hill to the back of the shack. I said a silent prayer of thanks that my family had taken me hunting so often as a child. They had instilled in me methods of moving through the woods with a minimum of noise. I reached the weathered gray rear wall of the shack and crouched there a moment, listening. At first, all I heard was my heart banging in my ears, then slowly other sounds returned; birds chirping, leaves rustling as they slowly twirled down from the canopy above, the far-off murmur of traffic on the main road. Then...a sound, a human one. A faint muttering, mumbling sound. I cocked my head, listening. It was coming from around the shack, from Buck's house.

Slowly, I crept to the edge of the rear wall and peeked around it. Buck's house sat sullenly in the clearing, the pickup truck listed gently to one side. Smoke curled lazily out of the chimney and drifted down toward the ground before slowly ascending. Between the sugar shack and the house, at the edge of the driveway, a stack of split wood filled the space between two trees. It was a hefty pile, probably some twelve feet long and eight feet or more high. Buck's heating source. I eyed the house a moment longer, the mumbling and muttering still going on. A television set? I cocked my head, listening intently.

It just didn't sound like that. It sounded like Buck.

The animal tracks I had been following continued on down the hill toward the woodpile, then suddenly veered to the left. From there they went off in a churned up line across the stream. I saw something on the tree next to where it veered away, something out of place.

It was a bright red splash.

Oh, man. I did not like this, no sir, not at all. But still...I had to know. A peek and then leave. Buck would never know I was there.

I took a deep breath and hitched up my pack, then carefully slipped along the building and down to the front of it. I stopped, my heart knocking in my chest. No movement from the house. Squatting low, I scurried soundlessly, zigzagging from tree to tree until I reached cover behind the woodpile. I stopped next to the tree with the red splash on it. I pressed my index finger on it; it came away red with blood. Large drops splattered the leaves next to the cloven hoofed tracks, tracks that now had a huge spacing between them as if the owner of them were in a dead run.

Another tuft of white hair glowed on the leaves some ten feet away from me.

I could hear the mumbling clearly now, the sound definitely not a television set. It was Buck. And it was coming from the window closest to the pile of wood. I strained to hear it clearly.

"I'm sorry I'm sorry, I didn't wanna do it, surely you know I didn't wanna do it, I had to do it, I had to. He ain't to be trusted, he ain't. I didn't mean to do it, but you had to git outta here. I can't let you be coming round here no more. You gotta git away, git away. Once all a' this is done, you can come home again. We will have the whole woods to ourselves. It's for the best. Just stay away a while longer. I'm sorry, I'm sorry..."

What the heck? Who was he talking to, anyway? I peeked around the edge of the woodpile at the house. The woods were still around it; the stream burbled and sparkled in the gloomy light under the trees. It was getting late in the day and darkness was creeping in around the edges. If I didn't get going soon, I was going to be doing the trek back to the Paddy Waggin' in full darkness. But still...I really wanted to know who he was talking to. Dare I try to get a little bit closer?

As I pondered that, I heard a motor growling up his driveway, the clunk as the car bounced through the ruts.

Shit, shit shit! There was no cover other than the wood-pile I was behind.

Pinned down like a moth on a board, I pressed my back against the pile and held my breath.

From inside the house, the muttering stopped. I heard the creak of his door. I remembered the greeting he had given me. I wondered if he was about to extend that same greeting to whomever was bold enough to drive on up to his house like that.

I hoped the woodpile was good enough cover if the bullets started flying. My mother flashed through my mind, her drawn face at my showing up at home after tangling with Buster.

"It's not like you have a degree in dog catching," her voice reverberated in my brain.

The motor grew louder, just on the other side of the woodpile now. I heard a car door open, then close.

Sweat trickled down my face.

"Buck? Come on out now. We need to talk about some things here."

Chapter Thirty-Four

There was a long pause, then I heard the door to his house creak open.

"What you want, Alfred?"

"I need an update. Where are we at with our plan, Buck? And any luck getting ahold of Marley?"

"Plan's fine plan's good. We are getting there. I expect the old lady's gonna get out of town any day now. Them people are really mad at her for stealing their dogs. She's gonna leave, I know it."

"You've been telling me this for weeks now. I'm not sure this plan is enough. I think we may need to turn the heat up a tad, get them all cooking at a boil. And what about Marley? He come back yet?"

Buck dropped his voice to a mumble. "I ain't seen him in a long while, a long while."

"Well, if he isn't coming to you, then you need to go to him, understand? I gotta get him, Buck. He's important to these people. Without Marley, there's no guarantee they're gonna go through with this plan at all. No sir, no guarantees. You want to give up a hundred thousand dollars over that, Buck? Huh? Yeah, I didn't think so. I need Marley and I need this plan to move forward...now... not in a week, not in a month, now. We clear on that?"

My curiosity was getting the better of me. Who the heck was this guy? I began to edge toward the side of the pile, trying to peer through the stacked firewood. I glimpsed the blue door of a car, a gray clad arm. His face remained annoyingly obscured. I tried rising on tiptoes to look through the next row of wood. No dice. I began to sidle cautiously toward the tree holding up the pile.

"I ain't giving up nothin'. I done told you, I'll get them outta there, you just gotta give me some time. I grew up here; I know how these people are. You can't pressure them. Just like you can't pressure me!" His voice started to rise.

"Now Buck, no one is pressuring you. We just have a deadline, is all. You know we gotta get this done before October 15, you know that. We don't have that much time left now, do we?" The man's voice had taken on a placating tone. "Why don't you come downtown with me tomorrow and we will sign the papers on this place, show these people we are serious? You can trust me, no one is going to go back on you."

Reaching the tree, I crouched low to the ground and slowly peeked around it. The car blocked most of my view; but from over the roof, I could just see the face of the person Buck was talking to.

It was the City Slicker.

What the hell? Like, what was he doing out here talking like this to Buck? It made no sense.

Buck muttered something I couldn't catch. I drew back out of sight again, straining to hear.

"Buck, we have a deal here. And I expect you to hold your end of it up now. I can't keep putting these people off.

Tell you what, you bring me Marley before the week is over and I'll see if I can get an extension on the rest of it. Huh? Can you do that?"

"I don't rightly know. I dunno where that thing got off to. I can have a look around, but I ain't promisin' you nothing." Buck's voice was sullen.

"Tell you what. You think on this overnight and think hard, Buck. Because if you can't or won't do this, I got someone who will. And that someone isn't terribly worried if he brings him to me dead or alive."

"What? You can't hurt Marley! You promised!"

"And you promised me you could get ahold of him without harming him. So what's it gonna be, Buck? Do it yourself or leave it up to me?"

Buck's voice sounded strangled with pain. "Ah hell, Alfred. I'll git him, I swear, you just gotta give me some time here..."

"Time I don't have. The only way I can get more time is you come downtown tomorrow and sign those papers for me on this place so I have a guarantee you're serious."

Sign papers? On Buck's home? The Checker family had lived on this wooded hillside for generations. This made no sense, no sense at all. And what deal did Buck have with this devil?

"Jesus, Alfred, you know I'm serious. But I don't want to sign over my pappy's place, even if it's temporary. Look, how about I get that woman to leave now so you can take her place, alright? And Marley, I'll go track him down. I'll go tonight. But don't make me sign over my pappy's place to you, even just temporary, okay?"

Alfred swore softly. "Alright Buck. I'm giving one more day, 24 hours. You get both of those things done, otherwise we go down to Town Hall and you sign those papers. You clear on that?"

"Yessir."

"I'll be back tomorrow then." The car door opened and slammed shut, the motor turned over again. He creaked and thumped his way back out the door yard.

"Son of a BITCH!" Buck's voice was scratchy as he shouted. "SON OF A BITCH!"

From behind me in the sugar shack, the stillness was shattered as a dozen or more dogs started barking. The barks ranged from high pitched yapping noises to the deep baying sound of a hound dog.

"SON OF A BITCH!" Buck shouted again. Faintly over the din, I heard the door to his house slam.

Son of a bitch was right. Buck nailed that one on the head.

Son of a bitch.

Chapter Thirty-Five

Despite my terror and the growing darkness, I tried to look inside the shack before I left, but there was no place to peek in. The door sported a large padlock and hasp, both new. The walls were windowless thanks to sheets of plywood nailed up over the existing windows.

One thing at least, the din from inside the shack covered up any noise I might have made. With a last worried glance down at Buck's house, I scurried up over the ridge behind the sugar shack. Once out of sight, I stopped for a moment to catch my breath and think about what I had just heard. That wasn't right, not right at all. It sounded like Buck was being blackmailed by this guy. Who was he? And what did he want from Buck? Who or what was Marley? The "old lady" he referred to was that Prudence? And holy cow; it sounded like Buck had fifty dogs in there.

I had to tell Uncle Jim, and tell him fast. I started trotting toward my car when the realization hit me that I couldn't tell Uncle Jim, not at least without admitting I had trespassed and spied on Buck.

Which meant anything we had learned from this wouldn't be admissible in a court of law should it come to it, the so-called 'fruit of the poisoned tree.'

I couldn't even tell Uncle Jim I had been here.

Shit!

The sky had darkened and the first stars were coming to life when I emerged from the woods on Thatcher Lane again. I was sweaty and scratched up from the briars. My right ankle throbbed where I had rolled it on one descent.

I could be home watching television or be out with my friends if I had gotten a programming job instead. I wouldn't be broke. I wouldn't be getting beaten up by goats. My parents wouldn't be stressed because of me.

Unbidden, Roger came into my mind, his eyes gleaming as he looked at me in the early days, the way he used to be my best friend. The pain of his defection hit me like a ton of bricks again. Tears sprang to my eyes. I wiped them away savagely.

This was all his fault.

I thought about Uncle Jim, and how upset he would be with what I had just done. About how happy he was since Sandy had come into his life...

Sandy. Sandy Case. The bulldog tenacious reporter. The same Sandy who had no compunction about doing whatever it took to get the story. Sandy would listen to me, she wouldn't yell at me or order me to stay away from Buck Checker.

She would go after him.

And I would help her. She'd let me: I knew she would.

Wincing at my ankle, I hauled open the door to the Paddy Waggin' and crawled inside it. Fumbling my phone out of my pocket, I started scrolling through it looking for Sandy's number. Finding it, I dialed her.

It went to voicemail. I hung up without leaving a message and fired up the motor.

I had an idea of where Sandy might be tonight. With one last glance into the now pitch black woods, I headed down Thatcher Lane.

The radio was on, tuned to our local station, WBRN. As I headed onto Bollinger, the song ended and the local news came on. I heard the scratchy voice of Harvey Willis, the station's news man.

I was not paying much attention as he rattled off the day's going news with the schools and town. However, my attention was piqued when he started talking about the hurricane.

Shit! I had to get over to the school and set up crates for that tomorrow.

"Hurricane Greta has made a turn at the North Carolina coast and has tracked back out slightly over the ocean, strengthening into a Category 3 storm. Its current projected trajectory will take it right up the coastline to about the Hudson River, where it may turn north. If that happens, we could experience a potentially devastating event here in the Vermont hills with up to 20 inches of rain possible. Other tracks show it could turn east instead, which could put Long Island right in the storm's patch. Keep your dial here on WBRN 99.1 for the latest in up-to-date-weather and news. This is Harvey Willis signing off."

Huh. Twenty inches of rain? Now that could really suck. But still, we were so far inland it wasn't like it would be much other than that. And I had bigger problems on my plate now.

What in the world was Buck up to?

I headed toward the community college, hoping that I could catch Sandy after she was done with her evening journalism class. She was teaching it, something she had recently taken up.

I really needed some good old-fashioned journalism right about now.

Chapter Thirty-Six

I caught Sandy just as she reached her car.

I must have looked a sight when I came screeching in with the Paddy Waggin'. My hair was a tangle of leaves and frizz, I was hobbling when I jumped out of the front seat. Her eyes narrowed at the sight of me.

"Geeze, Rachel, what's wrong? Is it that damn goat again?"

I shook my head no. "Sandy, you gotta help me. I can't go to Uncle Jim, and there's something terrible going on. I know it."

The day was catching up with me. My words were tumbling out in a staccato jumble. All I could see was Buck, blood on the tree, the sound of all those dogs and the threats of the city slicker. I felt the pit in my belly.

Her eyes narrowed. "Climb in and tell me about it." She indicated the front seat of her car.

Twenty minutes later, she swore softly. "Shit. You're right, Rach. You can't go to Jim or anyone on the police force now. But there has to be someway we can legally get on his property to check that sugar shack." She paused a moment, a slightly baffled expression on her face. "So, um, what IS a sugar shack exactly? Is that like a love nest or something?"

Oh, man. Sometimes I forgot she wasn't from around these parts. "A love nest? For Buck Checker? Ew, Sandy! Don't make me think about that! No, this is where people boil sap to make maple syrup."

"I just can't get used to you folks out here. You mean you build shacks in the woods where you sit around boiling tree sap? What's wrong with Aunt Jemima syrup?"

"Jesus, Sandy, don't you ever say that in public around here. That'll get you run out of town pronto."

She smiled wryly. "I'm sorta surprised it hasn't happened already. So, tell me about this mystery man, the so-called city slicker. Where'd he come from? Where's he staying? What's he doing?"

I shrugged. "I dunno. My friend Amanda started talking about him this afternoon to me, said he came in the Crusty Tart, that he was a real tool. Then we saw him on Main Street. Looked like he got on the wrong side of Joe and his crew."

Sandy smiled at that. "That's great news. That means it will motivate them to find out anything they can about him. You said this guy gave Buck a 24-hour deadline to do something?"

I nodded yes. She glanced at her watch. "Then we don't have a lot of time here. Let me get moving on this."

"Wait, I want to help."

"Oh Rachel, I don't know. No, that would be bad. Jim would never forgive me. No, I think I best go solo here."

"You can't do that to me, Sandy! For one thing, you'd never be able to find Buck's place without me! If you drive straight in, he will shoot you. And there's a whole bunch of dogs involved. Uncle Jim told me you were afraid of them."

"Say what?" Her eyes narrowed into slits, glittering dangerously.

"Well, even if not the dogs, what about the big white animal in the woods? I'm from these parts and even I'm nervous about that."

She looked away out the window for a moment, then heaved a sigh. "Shit. You're right Rachel. God damn it all, you're right." She turned back to me, her face grim.

"But so help me God, if you get into one ounce of trouble, you get the hell out of this pronto, you hear? Jim won't forgive me for endangering you, not at all. I know his limits, and that's beyond them. You'll be my guide and my resource on all things animal. Period. You promise me?"

"Yes, of course. I promise Sandy. I won't get into any jams on this."

Chapter Thirty-Seven

"This is the last of them." Sweat glistened on Amanda's forehead as she slid the stack of wire crates toward me from the back of the Paddy Waggin'. Activity bustled at the normally quiet high school on this Sunday as volunteers hauled cots into the gym. The hurricane was still on track heading up the coast, although some models showed it hooking east once it reached Long Island. It was due to make a move one way or another by tonight or early tomorrow.

Even if it did turn east, we were going to be in for a rainy week.

Across the parking lot, I spied a familiar tousle of brown hair and a goatee as Brian helped with the cots. I paused a moment, looking toward him. I felt a warmth spreading through me.

"Hey! Hello? Earth to Rachel?" Amanda's voice broke my reverie.

"Huh? Oh yeah, right, sorry." I flushed as I grabbed the end of the stack of crates. Amanda already had the other side.

"Is that Brian I see you mooning over?" Her voice was teasing.

"I was not mooning over him."

"Were too."

"Was not."

"Oh, hey, here he comes. Let's see how you don't moon over him now."

"Shut up!" The flush spread up my cheeks.

"Hey Rachel. Amanda. Here, let me get those for you." He took the stack from us.

Amanda flashed me a sly smile.

"Shut up Amanda."

"She didn't say anything." Brian glanced over his shoulder at me, his gray eyes serious.

I heard a giggle from her.

"No, but she will. I'm just getting in ahead of the rush." I shot her a look, one she studiously ignored.

Brian loped into the gym, carrying the stack easily. Inside, noise bounced off the walls as people milled around, setting up cots and tables. Over on the far wall, our crates were laid out in a row. We had tarps protecting the floor beneath and tarp end walls to keep the commotion for the animals down.

Brian set the stack down and pulled the top crate off. He started unfolding it.

"Thanks Brian." I took one end and helped shift it into its rectangular shape. Beside us, Amanda was unpacking a box of food and water bowls.

"So, um, do you think anyone will bring animals here if we get hit?" Brian glanced at me inquiringly.

"Yeah, I mean I guess. Uncle Jim said the last time they had to evacuate people, some wouldn't go because they couldn't bring them. He said they would rather stay and weather a storm than leave them behind."

Brian nodded. "I wouldn't leave Roscoe." Roscoe was his family's cat. "If we had to leave, he'd come with us."

Amanda smiled at him. "I knew we liked you, Brian."

I flushed again.

His smile grew larger as he looked at me. "What's not to like, huh?"

I turned away to grab another crate.

I heard Amanda say to Brian, "So did you know that Rachel is maybe going to become the animal control officer here full time?"

I turned back to them. "Well, it's not..."

"Really?" Brian's voice rose slightly. "You'd be staying here in Brownville?"

Behind him, Amanda shot a little grin at me.

"I'm not sure. I mean, like I don't know what I'm going to do. And I have a degree in computer science. This is about as far removed from that as it gets. And they aren't paying me anything and there are no benefits..." I trailed off at the look on Brian's face.

He looked down at the floor. "So where would you go then?"

Where indeed? Good question. Certainly not to England, where Roger and Courtney were partying up a storm. I had doubts about ever having to sit down and work all day on a computer, anyway. As messy and at times painful as this job was, the truth was...I liked it.

And I had to find out what Buck, and the stranger were up to. That came first. I wondered what Sandy had done today.

Next to us, Jake Cowan, one of our firefighters, was

setting up the last cot in the row. His radio crackled to life as a tone came through. Everyone in the gym froze.

"Dispatch to all units, respond to a code 9 at 23 Thatcher Lane, repeat all units code 9 23 Thatcher Lane. First alarm being struck at 13:23."

I whirled to look at Amanda, my eyes wide. "That's Prudence Collin's place!"

Chapter Thirty-Eight

Smoke was billowing above the treetops as we careened from Bollinger onto Thatcher Lane. I was ahead of the fire department; Amanda and Brian hanging on for dear life as I pushed the Paddy Waggin' to the limit.

I could hear the sirens faintly behind me.

"Oh, no!" Amanda and Brian said almost simultaneously as Prudence's house came into view. Flames were pouring out from the windows on the upper floor and licking their way up the roof. The interior of the house glowed a satanic shade of red. Prudence was in the yard, screaming hysterically.

"Thank God she's out!" Brian shouted as I skidded to a halt in a cascade of dirt. We tumbled out of the car.

"My dogs! My dogs!" Her shrieks were raw.

I grabbed her arms and tried to pull her away from the building. The heat was already almost unbearable. "Prudence! Prudence! You can't! Come on!"

"No!" she shouted. Twisting violently, she tore herself

out of my hands and ran a few wobbling steps toward the building. "My dogs!" She pointed a shaking finger toward the roof of the attached shed where five dogs cowered. "Save them!"

Oh, holy hell. They were on the far side, furthest from the flames, but almost at the same level as the upper floor. How the hell did they end up there?

"Prudence, wait, just wait, the firefighters are coming; they can save them." I tried logic.

The window closest to them exploded with a pop and a shower of sooty glass. Flames erupted out of the now empty window frame. Prudence screamed again as the dogs scrambled to the far end of the shed roof before cowering down. They didn't have much time left; flames were already crawling across the peak of the ramshackle one story shed.

I cast around frantically, spied an old metal trellis toppled over into the brush.

"You guys! Help me!" I raced over and grabbed it, yanking hard as it reluctantly tore free from the underbrush.

"Rachel! Are you crazy? You can't do that!" Amanda's voice had risen to a high soprano at the last word.

Brian, however, had a grim look on his face. He grabbed the end with me and yanked hard. Together, we dragged it to the far peak and propped it up. I began to scramble up.

"What the hell are you going to do?" Brian shouted.

"I'll pull them off and drop them down to you."

The trellis was some five feet short of the peak. I reached with my right foot and found the very top of it. The sirens strengthened, but were still too far away. Scrabbling for purchase, I found the edge of the shingles and hauled myself up.

I came face to face with a small brown curly-haired dog

who cowered, the whites of his eyes showing. Behind him, another four dogs huddled, ranging from small to another full sized hound. One growled at me, his tail tightly tucked between his legs. The heat from the house hit me full bore here. The fur on the dog closest to me was already singed.

Adrenaline kicked in. I reached out and unceremoniously grabbed the scruff of his neck, hauling him off the edge. He kicked in panic as he swung free. In one move, I leaned as far over the edge as I dared, dropping him into Brian's waiting arms below. Prudence's shriek could be heard above the crackling roar as she took him from Brian, cuddling him in her arms.

One down.

The little Jack Russell terrier mix shivered but didn't protest as I grabbed him next. Brian was already waiting. He dropped safely into his arms, Amanda taking him from Brian. Beside her, Prudence was on her knees, sobbing into the fur of the first dog.

I turned back for number three and saw something terrifying. The roof a scant twenty feet from me was ablaze, the flames marching toward the dogs. My face felt blistered from the heat.

"Shit, shit shit.... come on fellow." I reached out to the little cocker cross, who was growling at me. His lips drew back, the whites of his eyes showing. He snapped at me, terrified.

I yanked my hand back. Beside him, a fat black lab cowered. I reached out and grabbed the flabby folds of skin on his neck, dragging him toward me unwillingly. The hound whined and spun frantically, crowding closer to me and away from the flames.

I felt slivers stabbing my knees as I crawled backwards with the protesting Labrador Retriever. His paws reached the edge of the roof, and I grabbed a back leg with one hand.

"Sorry, my man, but there are no options," I muttered as I heaved him over the edge.

I heard a thud and an "Ooff!" from below me. Glancing over, I saw Brian slowly sitting upright, the Labrador safe and on top of him. Brian looked like he had the wind knocked out of him.

The flames were licking closer; the sirens were sounding like they were finally on Thatcher Lane. The cocker cross decided I was the lesser of two evils as the red and yellow fingers raced across the rooftop. He pressed his trembling body into me. I spun and leaned as far as I dared, Amanda waiting for him as Brian staggered upright. She caught him and fell to the ground with him.

That left the massive hound, who spun and bayed in terror. The flames were mere feet from us when I heard a crack and a hissing roar. The main house was starting to crumble in on itself, sagging to the ground, pulling the far end of the shed with it. I saw the hound's terrified eyes and lunged for him, wrapping an arm around his neck. From the corner of my eye, I saw flashing red lights as the firetrucks roared into the yard.

The house sagged lower with a groan, a gigantic ball of heat enveloped me and the hound. Without thinking about it, I launched off the shed roof; the hound clutched to me.

I felt the impact into two bodies as I landed, Brian and Amanda breaking our fall. The hound kicked and broke free from me, racing to Prudence and the other dogs who had clustered around her.

The house collapsed completely.

I sat up dazedly as the firefighters came racing over to us.

"Rachel! Brian! Amanda! Are you okay? Come on, get away from here. This shed's gonna go. What the holy hell were you thinking?"

Hands caught us and lifted. I stumbled and caught myself as we were pulled away to the mercifully cooler side of the road. Prudence and her dogs were already there, Prudence in hysterics now.

"Rachel! Rachel!" The voice came from behind the trucks. Looking up, I saw Sandy Case racing toward me, her ever present bag banging off her thigh. "Jesus Christ, Rachel! What happened?"

Firefighter Cowan sat me down on the running board of the closest truck. "She just did something pretty gol darned stupid is what just happened! Jesus, girl! What were you thinking?"

"What were you thinking is right?" Uncle Jim appeared, his face tight. "Rachel, what the hell? They told me you were just up on top of that..." the shed collapsed just then, sagging sideways before sinking to the ground in a shower of sparks.

Prudence was huddled in a ball sobbing, her arms wrapped around her dogs.

"They were all on the shed roof." Brian's voice. "She did what she had to do. We couldn't leave them up there. She just did a super brave thing." He looked at me dazedly.

The fire chief came over. "The paramedics are here. Let them check them out. Are any of you hurt?"

Brian looked down at his legs. "I think I might have hurt my ankle."

Amanda shook her head no. "I think I'm okay. You need to check her out." She indicated me.

"I'm okay. This is nothing compared to Buster."

"Rachel. Look at your hands."

I looked down and finally saw the slivers of wood sticking out from everyplace, even from under my fingernails. Blood dripped freely and soot stained them. I felt everything go gray and fuzzy.

"Oh." I said before fainting.

Chapter Thirty-Nine

I winced as they plucked the slivers from my hands; the damage looking worse than it actually was. Uncle Jim kept trying to shove an oxygen mask over my face. I kept batting him away. Finally, Sandy grabbed him by the arm and said, "Come over here a moment. We need to talk." She hauled him away.

Brian sat next to me, his knee scant inches from mine. Amanda sat on my other side. Jeff Malone, one of the paramedics, gripped my hand firmly as he plucked the last slivers from it. I winced. Across the lawn, the firefighters vainly sprayed water on the flaming remnants of Prudence's home.

Jeff dropped the tweezers into the metal bowl with a clang. "I still say you need to be checked at the hospital."

I shook my head no. "I'm an adult and I am refusing."

He heaved a sigh. "Look, if it's money, I'm sure the town's workman's comp will cover it. You were acting as the ACO when you did that crazy, fool...incredibly brave... stunt." He shook his head. "That was stupid, but there isn't a man here who isn't applauding what you did today."

I flexed my now de-slivered hands gingerly. "Is Prudence okay?"

He looked over at her. "About as okay as you could be, I guess."

Prudence was still huddled with her dogs, her arms wrapped around the lab and the cocker mix as the others leaned into her.

"Are the dogs all okay?" I asked as the flames began to wither into steam from the hoses.

"Seem to be," Jeff replied. "Will you at least follow up with your doctor, then? Your mom would scalp me if she knew I didn't force you to go to the County Hospital."

Shit. My mom. Her face flashed through my mind after Buster; what would it look like after this one? I grimaced at the thought.

Brian was watching me closely. "What is it, Rach?"

"Mom."

Amanda grimaced.

Brian looked at the two of us. "What? What is it?"

Jeff shook his head. "Your mom ain't gonna be exactly pleased at this."

Amanda turned to Brian. "Her mom's been on her case to get a computer programming job. She's not too keen on some of the things Rachel's been doing for this job."

Brian looked at me. "How can she be mad at this? You saved all those dogs. There's no way they would have lasted until the fire trucks arrived. And who knows what Prudence would have done if you hadn't done that? She could have gone back in to try and save them."

Prudence walked up behind Brian just as he said that, the dogs in a phalanx around her. Her face was tear and soot stained, but more composed than she had been. "I would have, you know. I tried getting to them from inside, but it was too much too fast." Tears spilled from her eyes again.

I looked up at her as Jeff wrapped a blanket around my shoulders. "How'd they end up on the roof, anyway? And how'd the fire start?"

She shook her head. "I don't know. I was downstairs canning my tomatoes when I smelled smoke and they started barking like crazy. They were all upstairs. There was a weird noise around then too, like something sliding or being opened. I ran up the front stairs, but the hallway was a solid sheet of flames." Her voice broke as sobs began to shake her again. Jeff took her arm and guided her to a seat next to me on the back of the ambulance. The dogs clustered around her, leaning on her legs and lying across her feet. Reaching over them, he placed his fingers on her pulse.

Brian looked from her to me. "But how could they end up outside then?"

"There's a window on the back stair landing that opens right out onto the backside of that roof. It's the only thing I can think of; that it was open, and they escaped that way. But I swear I had it closed."

"Unless what you heard was it being opened." I said. I wasn't liking this development. Buck came to mind. He wouldn't do this, would he? And how could he get in there without the dogs barking like crazy?

Uncle Jim came back just then, with Sandy a step behind him. His face had flushed a dangerous shade of red. She looked slightly sullen and a lot stubborn.

Uh oh.

"You okay Rachel?"

I nodded.

He knelt down in front of Prudence then. "Ms. Collins? You up to talking to us a moment?"

She wiped her arm across leaky eyes. "I-I- guess so."

"Talk me through everything that happened today." He listened intently as Prudence stammered through the events leading up to the fire. As she wiped the fresh cascade of tears off her cheeks, he asked, "Have you had any problems with your neighbor, Buck?"

I looked up at Sandy, my eyes wide. She met my eyes and shook her head slightly, then touched her lips with one finger in a 'shush' gesture.

"Buck? He's never bothered me. Why?"

"I'm just trying to figure out if anyone might have an issue here."

"Not Buck, but that nasty little man's been bothering me nonstop."

"What nasty little man?"

Prudence wiped her eyes. "I don't know who he is, but I've never seen him before. Short, roly-poly kind of fellow, wears a suit, talks fast and rude. He came by last week, then twice since, once a couple days ago and once yesterday." She looked at Uncle Jim, alarm on her face. "Who is he? Did he do this?"

"Now, now, we don't rightly know here yet. Tell me about him. What did he want?"

"He was going on about being with a company that pays cash for old houses. Said he could make me an offer I couldn't refuse. But I refused him alright. This is my home. I'm not leaving for him or anyone! You think he was behind this?"

Maybe Uncle Jim wasn't saying so, but I sure as hell was thinking about it.

And by the look on Sandy's face, she was thinking about it, too.

Uncle Jim stood up, his face grim. "Prudence, if you're

up to it, can you come over to the station with me? I want to show you some photos, see if'n you can identify the one that's the man who's been coming by here."

Jeff closed the top of his kit shut as Uncle Jim said that. "She's okay medically far as I can tell here, Jimmy. You up for it, Mrs. Collins?"

She wrapped her arm around the neck of her hound. "I'm not leaving my boys alone!"

"You don't have to." Uncle Jim looked at me. "You have the Paddy Waggin' here?"

I nodded.

"Mrs. Collins, Rachel here will hang onto your dogs for you. We gotta find you a place as it is. May as well get working on that. You got anyone you want to call?"

She shook her head no.

I saw the pitying look cross Uncle Jim's face fleetingly. "Well, come on then. We'll get you set up with something while we get all this figured out. Rachel, take her dogs. And Sandy. Stay here, and stay out of everyone's hair, alright?" He gave her a hard look.

She gave him a brilliant smile. "Well, of course I will. You don't have to worry about a thing!"

He took Prudence's arm and helped her up.

"I need to get leashes to get them in the van." I said as I stood up.

Prudence shook her head. "No need. They'll do what I ask of them." She looked at me, tears spilling afresh. "That's how I know something happened to Luther. He never would have run away from home like that."

Chapter Forty

I loaded Prudence's dogs into the back of the Paddy Waggin'. The wet dog smell it always had was now commingled with the stench of the acrid smoke from the fire. I grimaced as I climbed into the front seat. Amanda covered her nose and mouth.

The adrenaline rush began to fade, leaving me with quaking limbs. I tried and failed to insert the key into the ignition. Brian caught my hand. Despite my shakes, a jolt unrelated to the trauma we had just gone through shot through me.

Roger's face flashed across my mind.

Why was everything always so confusing?

"Hey." Brian's voice broke my reverie. "Let me drive. You rest for a while." He clambered out and came around, gently urging me to slide across to the passenger side, up against Amanda.

I didn't fight it.

"What are we going to do with her dogs?" Amanda asked.

I covered my nose and mouth too, as the smell made my

stomach flip. "I'm going to bring them back to the kennel, and you know, I think I should give them all baths. Prudence isn't going to want them smelling like that, and I don't want the kennel smelling like this either."

Brian nodded in assent as he put the van in gear. "I like that idea. Do some good in a crappy situation. Man! That fire was crazy! How did it spread so fast?"

I shook my head grimly. "I don't know, but her place was full of junk. I don't know what's going to happen to her now, but I hope to hell she can get some sort of help."

Amanda nodded in agreement. "She hasn't been right since Kelly died." She looked over at me. "How are your hands feeling?"

I flexed my fingers gingerly, feeling the throbbing in them. "Let's just say I won't be doing any keyboard work for a while."

"When was the last time you did any?" Brian asked as he slowed to take the turn into the driveway at the Department of Public Works, where the town kennel was located.

I laughed, a bark more than an actual laugh. "Like.... when I had my final at school?"

He slowed the van to a halt in front of the low building that housed the animals we collected from time to time. "That was last spring." He turned the ignition off and turned to look at me. "So why would you want to go back to that when you aren't even doing it in the first place?"

Beside me, Amanda dug her elbow into my ribcage. I winced at it, shoving back against her.

Behind us, the hound began to bay mournfully, cutting off further conversation. I shoved Amanda again.

"Come on! Let's get them out of here!"

Their claws scrabbled and echoed off the walls of the kennel as we clattered inside. I flipped on the overhead lights with my elbow. The hound on a leash was pulling me forward, and I had the Jack Russell terrier cross clutched in my other arm. Amanda and Brian were similarly encumbered with dogs as we made our way inside.

The kennel wasn't fancy, but it was functional. Three dog kennels with inside and outside runs lined one wall; a stack of four stainless steel cages for smaller animals like cats were in a small alcove off the far end. Along the other wall were supplies stacked on shelves, a mop sink and my destination for today; an old porcelain bathtub pressed into duty for times we had to wash skunk sprayed dogs off. Yellowing windows dotted the wall over the tub and sink. A dull gray concrete floor scarred from years of use completed the look.

And today, as it usually was, it was empty.

"How do you want to do this?" Brian asked me.

"They can go together. Put the Lab and the brown curly-haired one in one run. The Jack Russell cross and the Cocker can go together. The hound is big enough that he should go alone in the last one."

The chain link mesh doors clanked and toenails scrabbled as the dogs cast around in their new spaces. They were still worked up after their close call. I started pulling down bowls for water and kibble.

Amanda crouched next to one of the runs, rubbing the head of the overweight Labrador Retriever. He panted and drooled, leaning into her hand.

Brian took two of the filled water bowls and placed them into the runs as I filled more. Loud slurping sounds filled the air.

Slowly, they began to settle down. I pulled blankets down and started spreading them on the low beds each run had. Amanda plugged the tub and started running water into it.

My head was throbbing.

Brian looked at me, concern evident on his face. "Hey. Why don't you sit down and chill? We can do this."

I looked at him. "Since when do you know how to bathe dogs?"

"I had Mr. BumBum growing up. He used to roll in poop all the time. My dog, my responsibility to wash him off."

"Mr. BumBum?" I felt a laugh threatening.

"Hey, I was like 5-years old when I named him, ok?" A grin crept into the corners of his mouth.

I caught Amanda casting a sly glance at me. I gave her a side eye.

Brian opened a kennel door and caught the little curly brown-haired dog who had been the first one pulled off the shed roof. He picked him up, the dog's tail thumping against his rib cage as a pink tongue flickered out across Brian's cheek.

"Eww, hey now! Watch that tongue, buster!"

The dog wiggled as he gently set him into the few inches of water Amanda had drawn. They began to scoop water and pour it over him, lathering him up. He wiggled and licked both of them multiple times. Amanda giggled.

"I think he likes it." She said to me.

"I would if I smelled like that. Man, house fires reek."

Brian grimaced. "What do you make of what she said? About the man coming around harassing her? Then this. This doesn't feel like an accident to me."

It didn't to me either, but I hesitated. I didn't want to say anything until I had a chance to talk to Sandy. I flashed back to Uncle Jim's face after she had pulled him aside to talk to him. What was that about?

Brian lifted the now sodden brown haired dog out of the tub. He wiggled and tried his best to lick Amanda's face as she toweled him off. I opened the run and caught the Labrador by his collar. He looked up at me with a nervous expression. "Come on, my man. It's ok." I stroked his head. He lifted his chin and gave a small wag with his tail.

"Let me help you lift him." Brian said. He reached under him from the other side as I put my arm under his belly. Our hands brushed again. Again, that jolt hit me. Geez.... I had almost died today, and I was obsessing about touching Brian's hand?

The Labrador let out a sigh as we lathered him up. He reached up and swiped his tongue across my cheek.

"So what do you make of what Prudence said?" Brian asked me.

I shook my head. "I have no idea what to think. It seems weird but her place was also a disaster before today. I was there recently and you couldn't even see in some of the windows."

Amanda closed the kennel door behind the freshly bathed brown dog, who began shaking himself off with a fervor. "I think I read someplace that people who become hoarders like that are suffering from a mental illness. I suppose losing her husband and daughter could have done that to her. I wonder why she didn't want to sell to that guy? If that were me, I wouldn't be able to take the money fast enough."

I shook my head. "The sense of having a home is a lot stronger than money. That home was the last stable thing she had. That and her dogs." Luther crossed my mind, her missing hound. "I wouldn't bet she'd be interested in selling it, well before today, I guess."

I thought about Buck Checker and the city slicker, Alfred. Buck was another guy who wouldn't want to sell his home and leave, not willingly at least.

What was going on here?

I had to find Sandy pronto.

Chapter Forty-One

I headed back to the high school, leaving five freshly washed dogs under Brian's watchful eye. Amanda had already headed home. I turned the smelly Paddy Waggin' toward downtown and the school. Glancing up at the sky, I noticed high wispy clouds, the precursors to the weather system coming in.

Frowning, I turned the radio on. I had forgotten about the storm, the reason we were at the high school in the first place. As I came to the intersection of Main and Elm streets, a special bulletin came on about the weather.

The storm was turning to track right up the Hudson River. Breathlessly the announcer warned of the potential for up to 20 inches of rain in Vermont, starting tomorrow night.

Looked like our shelter would be pressed into service.

As I swung into the high school parking lot, the news changed to local events. Prudence's fire was the lead story. I shook my head.

I really needed to find Sandy.

The parking lot was bustling with activity. I scanned the lot; no Sandy.

Maybe she was still at Prudence's. I turned back out of the lot and headed back toward Thatcher Lane.

I could smell it long before I saw it; the acrid smell burned the back of my throat. Lights flashed through the trees as the last truck on the scene watched over the smoldering ruin. My heart thumped when I saw the blackened pile. Prudence had lost literally almost everything she owned in this fire.

Sandy had parked over by the firetruck. I spied her messy hair as she poked around the perimeter of the pile. I pulled over and parked near the truck.

Firefighter Cowan was standing guard over a hose that still sprayed a mist across the pile. He looked around at me when he heard the car door slam.

"Hey! Rachel! Are you okay?"

I nodded and held up my scarred up hands, flexing the fingers gingerly. "I'm good."

He shook his head. "Damn girl. I should be chewing you out for that, but that was something else. Those dogs wouldn't have made it, you know."

I didn't want to think about that. A shudder ran down my spine. The breeze sent a gust of smoke across my face, making my eyes water. I swiped my face briskly with my hand as Sandy came walking toward me.

"You okay?" She asked upon reaching me.

"Yeah, yeah I'm good." My eyes continued to water.

She eyed me for a moment but said nothing. I looked over at the pile. "What were you looking for?"

She shrugged. "Anything that seems out of place, but honestly, with this place being such a shit show before the fire, I can't tell if I am finding anything or not."

I looked at her for a moment. "Have you investigated fires before?"

She nodded. "Yeah. When I was in Chicago, before my ex-husband lost his mind, I used to be sent out on the criminal arson stories for the Tribune. I helped get a couple of guys sent up."

The city slicker crossed my mind. "Hey, look Sandy, I need to talk to you about something."

She glanced over at Firefighter Cowan. "Sure. Walk with me."

We headed away from the truck and started strolling the perimeter of Prudence's yard. The barn was untouched by the flames. Stopping in front of it, Sandy glanced back at the firefighters, then tugged on the sliding door. It creaked and squealed, rolling open a couple of feet before stopping.

She stuck her head inside. "Geeze...would you lookit' all this junk in here? Holy crap."

The interior of the old barn was stacked to the rafters with stuff; barrels, buckets, bales of hay, furniture, empty dog food bags, and more. I shook my head. "Her house was the same way."

Turning to face Sandy, I said, "That's what I wanted to talk to you about. Something is going on with that city dude. He's trying to blackmail Buck and Prudence said he was here repeatedly, trying to make her sell to him. Now this." I gestured to the remains of the house. "Have you found out anything about him?"

Sandy gazed at the smoking house, her eyes narrowed. "I spoke to One Eyed Joe and April. They said this guy showed up a couple of weeks ago. Said he is staying at the motel out near the highway. They don't like him; said he's pushy and mean." She shook her head and laughed briefly.

"The last time bad people came to this town, it didn't end well."

She was referring to the two Russian mobsters who had appeared last year trying to make a score at the town's expense. They hadn't counted on the likes of Sandy when they tried to muscle their way around.

I shook my head. "I don't like this, not at all. Neither Buck nor Prudence would ever willingly sell their homes. It sounds like Buck is being forced to, and Prudence was being pressured. And what's up with the dogs? They are being stolen all over town, and people are blaming Prudence for it, but I think Buck has them. Why would he do that?"

Sandy gnawed on her thumbnail for a moment, her gaze intense. "You know what they say; follow the money."

"Huh?" I looked blankly at her. "What money?"

"Exactly. Neither one of them HAS much money. I mean, look at how Prudence was living. I haven't seen Buck's place, but it sounds like a real hole. I need to get up there."

"Is Uncle Jim okay with that?"

She laughed, "Let's just say he hasn't come around to seeing things my way yet."

I thought about the interaction I had seen earlier. "You asked him to take you up there, didn't you?"

She smiled wryly. "Yeah. Let's just say it didn't go well."

"You didn't tell him what I did, did you?" I felt my heart start knocking in my chest.

"Oh, lord no! No, that's not something he needs to know...ever. No, we have to get up there sooner than later. Do you think he will talk to us?"

I flashed back to the sight of the rifle barrel aimed at my face.

"Um. I doubt it."

She nodded. "That's kinda what I thought. But if he needs us, he will have to talk to us."

I cocked my head and looked at her. "Why would he need us?"

"When we are the lesser of two evils." She smiled sweetly.

Uh oh...

Chapter Forty-Two

"So, we good here?" Sandy's eyes glowed as she recapped her plan with me. "I'm going to go find out who this Alfred character is, do a dive into his background. Then we meet at the kennel tomorrow at noon and head over to Buck's. We will take your van. When we get there, we tell him we have to talk to him about Alfred. We warn him he faces arrest if he doesn't cooperate with us. And we will tell him Alfred has told the police that Buck set fire to Prudence's house."

I chewed my lower lip. I thought about Buck and what his potential reaction to this would be. There weren't any good options that I could see.

"I don't know, Sandy. Buck's kinda unraveling. I'm not sure he's going to react the way you think."

She waved her hand dismissively. "He'll listen. I wish Jorge was still around; he'd go with us."

Jorge had been Sandy's coworker at the paper last year. Following the enormous case they busted open, he had won a Pulitzer and had then been offered a job at the Washington Times. He had departed for the Capitol late in the spring.

I wished he was still around, too. He had at least some effect at slowing Sandy down sometimes.

I sighed. "Okay. If you're sure this will work..."

Her phone trilled in her bag. "It'll work. He won't want to end up in jail." She started rummaging in the depths of her bag.

I wasn't sure, not at all, but I had nothing better to offer, either. We had to get Buck to talk to us about the dogs and the City Slicker, who appeared to be blackmailing him. If we could get him to open up, we had a decent chance of unraveling what was going on.

Sandy ended her call and dropped the phone back in the bag. "Gotta run. That was Russ over at the paper. He wants me to get ahold of the water commissioner. Apparently, there's some concern over the Blackwell Dam upriver."

"Huh." I replied, "That dam has been ancient since I was a little kid. It's always withstood everything, though."

She adjusted her bag on her shoulder. "They are saying this storm is going to be bigger than Irene was in 2011. More rain for one and now the potential for high wind too."

I felt alarm beginning to creep in. I remembered Irene. For all of my brave words to Uncle Jim, that storm had been catastrophic.

"If that dam goes, everything along the Sawmill River will get wiped out. And it goes right through Main Street."

Sandy nodded wryly. "Yeah, I am well aware of where the river goes." She had almost drowned in it last year. She frowned. "Has anyone warned One Eyed Joe about this?"

"I don't know. Uncle Jim has said nothing about it to me."

Joe and his crew lived along the banks of the river where it went through town. I thought about the channel it had; narrow and banked with stone embankment walls for a lot of the way. I wondered how they would fare if the flow suddenly increased one hundredfold. It wasn't a comforting thought.

"Gotta run. I'll see you tomorrow, okay? High noon, partner." She gave me a thumbs up. I smiled wanly and gave her one back.

I wasn't feeling too certain about any of this.

Chapter Forty-Three

The brilliant blue skies of the day before had disappeared under a sullen gray blanket. I frowned at the sky as I left the house for work. It was looking more and more likely we were going to get hammered in the upcoming storm, currently a Category 3 off the coast.

My phone buzzed as I settled into the Paddy Waggin.'

Roger.

My heart gave a sudden thump as the phone buzzed in my hand.

I hadn't spoken to him in months. Thought about him constantly, yes, but not spoken to him. My thumb hovered over the green answer button.

A text pinged in, pausing my thumb.

It was from Brian.

"Hey, wondering how you are doing? Hands ok?"

The phone stopped vibrating.

I sat there a moment longer staring at the glass face of it. What were the odds? That Roger would call me and Brian would text me almost simultaneously.

What the heck did Roger want? As far as I knew, he was still in England.

I realized then I hadn't looked at his social media in a long time. Events had simply been too much for mooning around over him.

I felt a pang of relief.

I answered Brian, "They're good, thanks."

His reply was swift. "Good. Need help at the shelter during the storm?"

A voicemail message popped up. Roger.

Ignoring it, I answered Brian instead. "I might. I will txt you if it looks like it, k?"

I tossed the phone in the cupholder without listening to Roger's voicemail. I had to take care of Prudence's dogs at the shelter, then stop by the high school to make sure everything was ready.

Then it would be back to the shelter to meet Sandy at noon. My stomach did a slow roll at the thought of confronting Buck.

My phone buzzed again. Dang it all! Was this Roger again?

It wasn't; it was Uncle Jim. And he sounded stressed.

"Rachel, you gotta get over to Morton's farm. They were trying to move everything up out of the flats by the river and they done busted through the fences. He's got livestock and birds all up and down the road, and his boys aren't there; they're up to the city for the day."

"Ugh. Okay, I'll get over there. "

"Look, you got anyone else you can call to help? It's just you and Cyrus as of this moment. I'd go, but the Chief just told me there's a call over to Victoria Street I have to go to."

Brian flashed through my mind. "Yeah, maybe. Let me try a couple of people."

"Okay, thanks. Hey how are Prudence's dogs?"

"They were okay as of last night. I was heading that way now, but I might call Damion to go instead."

"Okay, great. And Rachel? Be careful, okay?"

I assured him he had nothing to worry about and signed off. I texted Brian and Amanda, asking them if they could help with Morton's. Both answered immediately and in the affirmative. I glanced at the icon showing Roger's voicemail and tossed the phone back in the cupholder again without listening to it.

Morton's farm was down in the river bottom between the Connecticut River and River Road. As I headed down the last stretch to the farm, I came across a roadblock.

I slammed on the brakes, halting the Paddy Waggin's in a shuddering cloud of dust.

About 50 head of black and white Holsteins were grazing and strolling down the road. Interspersed with them were birds of all description; Chinese geese, chickens in every color of the rainbow, about a dozen goats and another fifteen or twenty sheep. A shaggy donkey eyed me with mistrust as I clambered out of the van. On the other side of the herd, almost invisible behind the wall of livestock, I spied the orange hat of Cyrus Morton. He was swearing mightily as he tried to coax his lead cow back into the field.

It was like nailing jello to the wall.

I heard an engine behind me: a glance showed it was Amanda with Brian riding shotgun.

"Cyrus!" I shouted, "We are over here. Tell me what you want to do."

"Get these goldurned ornery critters back into the field on the left for now. I'll git 'em sorted once they's outta the road."

One of the goats made a sudden run for it, taking the

other goats and sheep with it. The cattle jumped and spooked in all directions and the geese started shrieking.

'Gol dang it all! I swear I'ma gonna make curried goat outta that one!"

Brian and Amanda reached me, both wearing grins. I glanced at them wryly. "Think it's funny, eh? Let's see how it feels in an hour or so."

I heard the ping of a text coming from Brian. He raised his wrist and eyed his wrist where a new tech watch gleamed.

"Oh, fancy. When did you get that?" Amanda asked.

"I just got it last night. It's weird, but it's useful too. I can answer my phone on it and reply to texts using my voice." He replied.

"Humph." I snorted. "You can barely use your phone at times, let alone that."

From across the milling herd of cattle, Cyrus swore with a heartfelt intensity as three cows suddenly made a break for the other side of the road, taking the remaining herd with them.

I felt a grin threatening.

"Come on, you guys. Let's give Cyrus a hand before he loses his mind here."

Forty-five minutes later, I wiped sweat from my face as the cows tromped away from us up the low hillside behind his barn. I heard a squawking and flapping of wings as Brian and Amanda herded the last of the birds into the enclosure next to the low slung red and white barn. The geese and chickens honked and clucked over the excitement they had just been through.

"Success!" Brian called out as he followed the last chicken into the run. Amanda closed the gate behind him. I sighed and leaned the shepherd's hook that Cyrus had given me for heading the birds back together against the outside of the enclosure. We still had the sheep and goats to deal with, but they were spread out grazing peacefully in Cyrus's field, not in the road.

I heard the ringing of Brian's phone from across the enclosure. He lifted his arm and looked at his wrist. He reached up and tapped the face.

"Hello?" He shouted at his wrist.

A snort of laughter snuck out of me. Across the enclosure, I saw Amanda doing the same.

From Brian's wrist came the tinny voice of Dominic, Brian's cousin. The speaker on the phone made it distorted and alien sounding.

From behind Brian, six geese all hissed in unison.

Uh oh...

Oblivious to the impending doom he faced, Brian started talking to Dom as the Chinese geese thrust their beaks in the air and clustered together behind him. Dom replied to Brian, his voice rising, amplified by the tinny speaker.

The geese began to screech in alarm. As one, they turned and started half running and half flying at Brian, wingtip to wingtip across the enclosure.

Oh snap...

I grabbed the shepherd's hook and vaulted over the top of the fence. Brian, belatedly realizing he was about to be assaulted, turned to see the avian equivalent of a heat-seeking missile locked and loaded on him.

He gasped and backpedaled away from them as Dom droned on, oblivious to the peril he had just put Brian in.

I reached Brian a moment before the geese did.

"BACK!" I whooshed the hook across in front of me like a scythe.

They screeched in unison.

From Brian's wrist came, "Whaaaa? What was that?"

The geese hissed again.

"Brian! Hang up the phone!"

He was staring at the geese in horrified fascination.

"Brian! Hang it up!"

Dom replied, "What's going on over there?"

A tan goose snaked his neck at me, clattering beak narrowly missing my kneecap.

From the other side of the fence, I could hear Amanda. She was laughing hysterically.

"Brian! Hang. Up. The. Phone!"

He finally reacted, slapping his wrist and silencing the tinny voice.

"Back!" I threatened the geese with the hook as they clustered together, unsure of their next move.

Finally, they waddled away, chattering among themselves about the danger they had just chased away.

Brian's phone rang again.

"Don't you dare answer that!" I called to him. Behind us, Amanda gasped for breath, tears of laughter rolling down her face.

Keeping a leery eye on the retreating geese, we exited the pen.

Technology. It was going to be the death of us all one day.

Chapter Forty-Four

The sound of rain lashing my window woke me at 5:00 a.m. Blearily I sat up to peek out at a rain washed world. I heard my father stirring in the kitchen, so I kicked back the covers to go join him. My phone glowed on the bedside stand; Roger's voicemail was still unheard. I stared at it for a moment, wondering why I had this weird reluctance to hear what he had to say? Was it because I was afraid of what he would say, or afraid of what he might not say? All I knew was as long as I left it unheard, I had more time to deal with the aftermath.

I had just swung my feet down to the floor when my phone started trilling again. I glanced over at it: Brownville Dispatch. With a grimace, I grabbed it to hear Sergeant Dexter, one of the night shift cops, on the other end.

"Rachel, we need you over here, stat. We got a call that Meredith Malloy's coop is in danger of getting washed into the water. She needs help getting her chickens evacuated."

"The crazy chicken lady? Where am I supposed to take them?" My mind flashed back to the chicken dressing games she was playing the day I was over there. Good Lord, she must have thirty birds, at least. "We can't take them to the high school."

"I know, I know, how about just getting them corralled and we can figure it out after? Maybe the kennel, if you have to?"

"Not with all of Prudence's dogs still there."

"Look, the phone's ringing again. Go help her and we will figure it out, ok?"

I grabbed my clothing from the day before and charged downstairs, grabbing a cup of coffee as I ran through the kitchen. My dad looked up at me, his hair standing every which way on his head.

"Where are you off too, so early?"

"Mrs. Malloy's over on Searles Cross Road. I have to evacuate about thirty chickens and God only knows where I can put them after."

My father set his newspaper down on the table and looked at me a moment. "I bet my buddy Ernie would let you put them in his old shed out back. I'll give him a ring if you want."

"That would be great, thank you. Just warn him that Mrs. Malloy is a little...different."

My dad grinned. "Maybe I will wait to tell him that. And Rachel...be careful out there today. This storm isn't anything to sniff at, you know. Let us know what you're up to today, okay? Your mom...she's still pretty upset about the fire at Prudence's."

Upset was sort of an understatement. Mom had almost blown a gasket when she heard what I had done. Small towns were not known as being good places if you wanted to keep a secret. I don't think an hour had passed before she heard four different versions of what happened.

I snagged a banana and the keys to the Paddy Waggin'. "I'll be careful Dad. I won't do anything rash."

My intended meeting with Sandy later today flashed through my mind. Crud...the rain had started earlier than we realized it would. I said goodbye to dad and pushed my way out the back door.

My windshield wipers left large streaks across the glass, and the wet dog smell was worse than usual as I splashed my way across town to Mrs. Malloy's house. The air was hot and muggy, with rain sheeting across the roadway. I spied her little house, the normally tranquil Punch Brook behind it splashing above the banks. Her chicken coop listed on the embankment, the earth swirling away down the brook at an alarming rate. Mrs. Malloy was out in the yard, gray ringlets stuck to her head, her glasses spattered with rain. Chickens scurried around her feet, many of them trying their darnedest to get back out of the rain and back inside the coop. She shrieked as she tried to stop them.

Oh boy.

I parked and raced across the yard as she emerged with two struggling hens under her arms. I realized that part of the moisture on her face was from her own tears. She was sobbing almost uncontrollably. I reached for her and grabbed the two hens. "Mrs. Malloy! You can't go back into that coop! It's too dangerous!"

Her answer was to turn and run back into it. Oh, no...I turned and sprinted to the van, where I tossed the two hens in unceremoniously. She was emerging from the coop with an armful of chickens when I reached her again. "I still have about five girls in there!" She shouted as she thrust wet birds into my arms again. My hands stung under the bandages as the hens kicked and struggled in my arms. I staggered for the Paddy Waggin'. I heard a cracking noise behind me. I glanced over my shoulder to see the back corner of the coop hanging loosely over empty space, the footing beneath it racing away down the brook.

Crap! I fumbled for the van door with the five hens I held kicking and shrieking. A wing cracked me in the face. Sliding the door back, I jammed them into the space and slammed it shut. Feathers swirled soddenly toward the ground. I raced back to the coop. She was still inside.

"Mrs. Malloy! Mrs. Malloy! You have to get out! Now!"

She shouted something unintelligible as the coop began to list backward toward the brook. I shouldered the door open into the low-ceilinged space and saw her on her hands and knees. She was trying to get under a nest box where two hens cowered, three others clutched in her arms.

I grabbed her arm and tugged. "I'll get them! Get out now, get them to the van!"

She backed away, sobbing.

Crap, crap, crap. From my right, the light from the washed out bank lit the interior of the coop. A pair of Golden Comet hens were pressed flush to the back wall, silent and terrified. I dropped to my hands and knees and crawled into the muddy space. There was another crack as the coop listed further.

My fingers brushed feathers. I latched hold of the first hen by her wing. She didn't scream, but she started kicking and struggling. The second one cowered and tried to crawl further away. I dropped onto my belly and grabbed blindly at her. I felt a scaly leg and started scrambling backward on my knees, a hen in each hand.

There was an enormous crack from over head. The coop, already ancient before this, was finding the stress of moving earth to be too much for it. The back wall sagged down into the water and the roof started tipping toward the brook. I scrambled backwards with the two terrified hens in my hands, my feet kicking behind me, searching for the doorway.

From outside I could hear Mrs. Malloy's shrieks as I backed out of the small opening, an opening that was suddenly growing larger as the coop tipped further toward the now raging Punch Brook. The hens struggled and flapped, mud ground into my knees as a groan filled the air. The coop, now resting on air on the back third, gave into gravity with a moan.

The water pulled it into the current in a swirl. I stared as it bobbed and floated down the river, first crashing into one bank, then the other. Beside me, Mrs. Malloy cried and wailed.

"My coop! My coop!"

The other hens were clustered on her screened in back porch in a silent, wet clump. Rain lashed down, soaking my hair to my head and soaking my clothing.

"Are you okay?" I shouted at her. She nodded, the water spraying off her head. "Come on, let's get your girls into the Paddy Waggin'. My dad said he would call your neighbor Earl. He thinks you can use his shed for now."

I put the two hens I held into the Paddy Waggin' and pulled it over closer to her porch so we could transfer the rest into it. The smell of wet chickens filled my nose.

A quick call to my dad confirmed the use of Earl's shed, so I headed over there, Mrs. Malloy following along behind me. My phone rang as I pulled into his driveway: dispatch calling to tell me there was another emergency, this time on the Sawmill River. Silas Dunham's yard was underwater, and Silas and his three dogs and two goats needed to get out of there.

My phone never stopped ringing. After helping Silas

evacuate, I headed over to downtown for a report of a loose dog running around the center, dodging in and out of traffic. As I wrangled him, I cast a leery eye on the Sawmill River, which was already angry and swollen. The rain came in bands, each one harder than the last, and around 2-o'clock, the wind, which had been mercifully absent, started lashing the town and the surrounding hills and fields.

And still the storm related calls came in. Roads washed out, more ramshackle sheds collapsed under the onslaught, more frantic calls came into dispatch for help.

I was completely worn out when I let John and Lucy Gray out at the high school shelter, along with their two cats and one dog. A breach in the bank of the Sawmill River had cut them off, forcing them to leave their car on the far bank. They needed a ride to the shelter after evacuating their home. I wasn't sure they were going to have a home to go back to; my headlights had shown the normally placid river had turned into a brown maelstrom of surging water and debris.

And the worst was yet to reach us.

With a nervous glance at the darkening skies, I turned the wheel toward home and my own bed.

Chapter Forty-Five

The television woke me up around 6:00 a.m. Dad was in the living room with it tuned to the weather channel. The floorboards were cool beneath my feet as I swung my legs over the edge of the bed, yawning and rubbing my eyes with my fists. They felt like they were filled with grit.

My phone started buzzing on the nightstand. Without looking, I snagged it. This early, it had to be dispatch.

"Hello, Rachel here."

"Rach? Rach, it's me, Roger. How are you?"

Roger? Oh holy hell. I had completely forgotten about the call yesterday in all the chaos. What could he possibly want? I hadn't spoken to him in like three months now.

"Rachel...are you there?" I realized I was sitting there mute.

"Uh...yeah, yeah, I'm here. What's up?"

"I.... I just wanted to say hi, that's all. I miss talking to you."

"You miss talking to me? I'm sorry, but weren't you the one who dumped me and went to England? I think you stopped talking to me first." I wasn't at my best before my morning tea.

Or come to think of it; maybe I was this time.

I heard him sigh. "I know, I'm sorry. That wasn't very nice of me. I've missed you though, missed you a lot."

Despite myself, I felt a little flutter. Stammering slightly, I asked "Where are you?"

"I'm still in Cambridge."

"Why are you calling so early?"

"Um, it's almost lunchtime here? We are five hours ahead of you. Oh, I'm sorry! Were you still in bed?"

"No, I was getting up for work, anyway."

"Um, so what's up with you?" He asked me.

I looked out the window where the rain was lashing the panes in wind driven streaks.

"We have a crazy hurricane hitting us now. They're saying we are going to get hit hard."

I heard a familiar snort come from 3,000 miles away. "A hurricane? Rachel, it's Vermont. You don't get hurricanes there. I mean, a little rain and maybe some wind, but not like it is down south."

Outside, I heard a crack as a limb on the old maple tree by the road let go. My phone vibrated as a second call came in. This time, I looked at the screen; dispatch.

"Look, Roger, I have to take this call." I moved my thumb to end our call.

"Rachel! Wait! I need to talk to you about something. It's important."

"I'm sorry, but I can't, not now anyway. Roger, I have to go." I ended the call and hit accept for dispatch.

It was Uncle Jim.

"Rachel, have you seen Sandy? Ah can't reach her and her landlady says she never came home last night."

Our plan flashed through my mind, the plan I had completely forgotten for yesterday.

Sandy! Shit!

Oh shit.

"Rachel? You there?"

"Yeah, I'm here."

"You know what she's gotten herself up to?"

I closed my eyes and covered them with my left hand. Oh shit. He was not going to like my answer one bit.

"Rachel? You aren't saying anything. Do you know where she got herself off to?"

I said a silent prayer.

"Yeah Uncle Jim. I do..."

Chapter Forty-Six

I grabbed at the door handle to steady myself as Uncle Jim swerved around a downed tree in the road, his tires screeching in protest at the move.

"Ah cain't believe you two cooked this fool scheme up in the first place, never mind that you wouldn't let me know what was happening! That Buck ain't wrapped too tightly, Rachel! What in God's name were you thinking, letting Sandy go up there?"

The car slammed through a washout in the dirt road, sending a jolt through my teeth.

Outside it was Armageddon. The wind had arrived with a vengeance. Limbs, power lines and even utility poles leaned or were downed all around us. I saw a large tree on the roof of the Mayfield's place as we roared by.

Uncle Jim's radio crackled nonstop with emergency calls. The most pressing one was that the hydroelectric dam several miles upstream had had to open the floodgates to avoid losing the plant. The Blackwell Dam was now in imminent danger of collapsing, with raging water topping it.

The police and fire departments were frantically evacuating people anywhere near the waterways.

I held onto the door as Uncle Jim slewed around a corner at speed, the car sliding on the mud.

The turnoff for Buck's driveway was just ahead.

I looked across at Morton's farm, where we had just herded all of his animals out of the road a scant 48-hours ago. The normally peaceful river had stormed its banks, turning Cyrus's fields into brown lakes. His house and barns stood untouched on higher ground. They had deliberately built it that way almost two hundred years ago by his forbearers when they discovered how the river acted when it flooded.

I thought about our destination, Buck's place, and how his house and sheds were on the banks of the Sawmill River, a river that was already over its banks. If the Blackwell went, he was in deep trouble.

And if she was there, there was a really good chance that Sandy was too.

I pushed that thought away. She couldn't be there, she simply couldn't be. I had gotten no calls from her yesterday. Maybe the paper had sent her after a story instead?

I had tried to bring that up to Uncle Jim. His jaw was set.

"Ah called over there. They ain't seen her either."

We skidded around another turn, the car wallowing in the mud, then Uncle Jim slammed the brakes on full. The dirt road was gone, washed out by a side stream turned raging river. Buck's driveway was a scant quarter mile up the road. Uncle Jim swore a heartfelt one.

"Rachel! I'm going in on foot. You stay in this car and call the captain, let him know what I gotta do. You stay out of this now, you hear me?"

"Uncle Jim! You can't do that!"

"Yes, Ah can and Ah will. Now you call the Captain and you wait for him, you got it?"

I looked at the washed out road. "How are you going to get over there?"

Uncle Jim nodded to his left. "Morton's got a cross over in that field. Ah can get across on foot."

Leaning forward I spied the wet logs barely visible above the surging water. "You're going to walk across on that?"

Uncle Jim was reaching into the back seat. He came up with a rifle. "Ah can and I'm going to. Call the Captain; Ah ain't got time!" He slipped out the door and slammed it behind him. I saw the rain lashing him.

"Uncle Jim! You can't do this! It's suicide!"

He paid me no attention, heading across the field to the makeshift bridge at a trot.

I held my breath as he inched out on the slippery logs. Reaching the other side, he jumped down into the brush, disappearing momentarily before reappearing on the road on the other side of the brook. He gave me a wave and headed out at a fast trot.

I grabbed the radio, fumbling slightly with it. Keying the microphone, I tried calling the station. Static answered me.

"Damn it all!" I tried again, tried different channels. Still, nothing. I realized then that all I was hearing now was static; no more calls were coming through. I pulled my cell phone out and thumbed it on.

The upper right corner showed no bars at all.

I realized then that this probably meant the tower on Lunt Hill was down; it carried cellular and police communications.

"Shit!" Uncle Jim had disappeared.

Frantically, I cast around. I couldn't let him go into Buck's with no backup. That meant I had to follow him in. With shaking hands, I undid my seatbelt, preparing to slide out and follow his path across the precarious log bridge. As I did so, motion caught my eye; the end of a log rising skyward as the water took the bridge down.

"Oh no! No!"

The logs bumped and tumbled past me in a swirl of brown water.

"No!" I pounded my hands on the dash in frustration.

Now what?

I realized the best way in would be to go around to the back of his property, the way I had gone in a million years ago. If the storm hadn't closed it, Parker Road would hook over and join just south of Bollinger, where Prudence's house was. The hill behind Buck's was high ground; I could probably get over that pretty quick. I pushed away the thought of the trees on it; I couldn't do much about those coming down except to keep moving and to keep an eye peeled. I'd rather take my chance with trees over water, anyway.

The dogs crossed my mind.

If they were still in that shed, I would break them out. There was no way Buck would hear the noise over the storm.

I tried the radio once more. Static answered me.

With a muttered prayer, I slid over into the driver's seat of Uncle Jim's cruiser and put it in drive.

Chapter Forty-Seven

The sky was an eerie shade of greenish gray as I flew over Parker Road. Branches littered the surface and tree tops danced in the roaring wind. My fingers were bone white from the grip I had on the wheel.

It was like the world had ended. I didn't see another vehicle on the roads, nor any people. No lights shone through the gloom. Every culvert was overflowing and angry. Every place I had to cross water was nerve-wracking.

I wondered if I should head to the police station instead, tell them what was happening. But tell them what, exactly? That Uncle Jim had raced into the storm, into Buck's because he thought maybe Sandy was there? They were probably stretched thin with the storm by now. No one would be able to respond to that.

But I couldn't leave him alone either. I pressed the accelerator as hard as I dared, the flashing lights on the roof reflecting back from windows and wet surfaces at me.

I skidded into Bollinger, then turned onto Thatcher Lane, stopping where I had parked a million years ago now.

I looked around the cruiser for a weapon; I was loath to go there with nothing.

There was nothing but Uncle Jim's flashlight, a heavy black affair. I grabbed it and pulled my coat tight around me before slipping out into the storm.

My hair whipped across my eyes before promptly matting down against my skull, wetted by the firehose of rain we were experiencing. The wind howled in the tree tips, which swayed and groaned under the onslaught. I cringed back for a moment, then sucked my breath in.

"Come on Rachel; just get there fast and get out."

I headed up the hill at a run.

I was glad for the years of playing sports in school, particularly track. I steadied into a fast lope, dodging rocks, logs and downed branches. I covered the backside of the hill far faster than I had crept up it before. Crossing the plateau on top, I paused momentarily before plunging downhill. From here I could see the dark back wall of the sugar shack and a glimpse of Buck's house. The normally peaceful little brook was anything but now. It sprayed and hissed, water shooting higher than the sugar shack. I knew it passed close behind Buck's house.

I prayed Sandy wasn't there.

I started to run down the hillside toward the sugar shack, heedless of the noise. There was little to no chance Buck would hear it over the storm, which now roared like a wounded animal. I leapt over a stone wall.... and pulled up short suddenly.

I heard voices over the wind, heard voices and saw... something. Something large, white and alive. Something that was tied to a tree on the edge of the driveway.

What the heck?

I crouched down and peered through the brush trying to make sense of what I was seeing.

Crab walking down the slope behind the shack, I cautiously peered around the edge. There was no sound from inside this time. Down alongside the driveway stood the same pile of firewood I had hidden behind. But this time, a huge white animal, larger than a horse or a steer, milled around the edge of the driveway, panicked by the rope halter that was cinched around its head. Peering closer, I realized...

"Holy shit! It's a freaking moose!"

I blurted the words out loud, so startled at seeing a giant white moose that I couldn't keep my mouth shut.

From the shack next to me, dogs erupted into barking. Dogs and something else...

"Hey! Hey! Shut up God damnit it! Hey, is anyone out there? Help! Shut up, you fools!"

Sandy!

I ducked back behind the shack as Buck appeared in the driveway. He was hatless and wild-eyed, his long gray hair plastered down on his head. I heard a voice, not Buck's, at the same time.

"Don't you mind those damn dogs! I'm telling you now, you give me that title and this damn critter or you're going to join your ancestors. I'm done messing around here, Buck!"

I knew that voice.

Peeking around the shack again, I caught a glimpse of a blue suit and a hand that was holding a gun pointed right at Buck.

Oh crap!

Buck turned and yelled at the city slicker, aka Alfred, "You ain't killing Marley! You promised!"

Alfred scoffed, "You aren't exactly in what I would call a bargaining position here, Buck. I told you, I got people who will pay good money for his hide on their wall and I intend to collect. And speaking of collecting, you reneged on your promise to deliver those properties to me. I had to do the deed myself and burn that old lady out of her house. I'll do that to you next!"

Holy shit! He had burned down Prudence's house!

Next to me, I heard the dogs still barking, and then Sandy's voice, "Who's out there? For God's sake, get me out of here!"

I ducked further behind the building and scanned for a way in. I saw a knothole in one board along the back. I leaned over next to it as the wind roared and limbs thudded to the ground a short way up the slope from us.

"Sandy! Sandy, it's me, Rachel!"

"Rachel? Ah shit..."

"Hey!" I was stung by that.

"No, no, I was hoping you were Jim."

I glanced around, seeing nothing but storm lashed woods. "He's around someplace, but I don't know where. Hang on, let me try something here..." I had spied a potential way in. A board on the back wall was warped and sticking up, the weathered ends punky and gray. Nails hung in the air instead of in the wood. I grabbed a chunk of wood off the ground as the dogs set up a racket again.

"For the love of God, shut up!" Sandy bellowed from inside.

I jammed the edge of the branch into the gap as another branch thudded down off the roof of the shack. I jumped and cringed at it.

"Hurry up! I got to get out of this shit hole!"

The wood cracked as I pried on the branch. From inside

I caught a glimpse of Sandy's face, wide eyed and dirt streaked. A dog's nose thrust itself into the opening next to her, causing her to jump back. "Get out of there! Me first! Me! God, Rachel, hurry! It's pitch black in here."

I realized I still had Uncle Jim's flashlight in my inside coat pocket.

"Sandy, wait..." I tugged it free and shoved it in the opening butt first. "Here. Take this."

"Oh, thank God!" Light bloomed off her face.

I shoved on the piece of wood harder, working the small opening into a slightly larger one.

"Give me something to work with and I'll help." I cast around, finding another chunk of wood that I passed through to her.

"What happened?" A piece of wood splintered. Over the wind and the dogs, I could hear the voices rising.

"What happened is Buck is bona fide nuts, that's what happened. When you didn't show up, I came down here anyway. He met me with a shotgun and shoved me in here. He didn't care one bit about the police or anything. He just kept muttering about someone named Marley, that no one was going to kill Marley."

"Yeah, well, Alfred is trying to kill either Buck or Marley right now."

"What?!"

A piece of wood snapped.

"He's down there with Alfred and he has a giant white moose, who is Marley by the way, tied to a tree, and Alfred has a gun on him. You gotta get..."

I heard the loud pop of the gun.

Chapter Forty-Eight

"Shit!" I dropped my piece of wood.

"Rachel! You get out of here. I got this."

"Like hell. Hang on."

I crept to the edge of the shack and peered around the edge of it. The scene below brought me up short. Alfred had moved closer to Buck, only now he had his gun trained on something else. Someone who was now sprawled in the driveway, the rifle he had carried lying several feet away from his outstretched hand. Uncle Jim grimaced in pain and clutched his left calf, red blood showing under his fingers.

Buck's mouth hung open as Alfred stepped closer, taking aim at Uncle Jim.

"Uncle Jim!" I shrieked and leapt out from behind the shack. Behind me, I heard Sandy yelling.

Alfred spun around, bringing the gun to bear on me as I careened off the hill and around the firewood into the driveway. "Uncle Jim!"

Buck jumped toward Alfred. "Don't you dare hurt her! I swear I'll kill you if you try it!"

To my right, the moose leaned backwards against the halter on its head, the tree leaning and cracking under its weight, its eyes rolled back, showing the whites as he strained. Uncle Jim met my eyes. "Aw damn it all, Rachel! Ah told you to stay in the car!"

I started toward him, only to have Alfred step into my path, the gun leveled at my face. This close, the barrel was huge, the hole like a sewer hole scant feet from me. There was no way he would miss at this range.

Behind me, I heard the dogs barking and Sandy's yells mixed in. Uncle Jim heard her too.

Alfred kept the gun on me but spoke to Buck. "I'm not doing anything to this one. But you are. You and her are going in that shed with those dogs. I'll deal with this one myself."

I realized he didn't know Sandy was up there. Uncle Jim realized it at the same time. He started shouting at Alfred to cover Sandy's yells.

"Shut up!" Alfred yelled at him, but kept the gun steady on me. "If you bumpkins had just kept your end of the deal, I'd be long gone. But noooo...someone had to get all mushy over a damn animal. That thing is gonna look great on the wall."

"You can't hurt Marley!" Buck's eyes glowed behind his smeared glasses as he shouted at Alfred. "I done raised him from a calf! Bottle fed him and everything! You told me you were only gonna use him to get them people from the lab to buy Prudence's place! That you were gonna tell them he was special, that her land is special and perfect for their lab!"

"Oh, he's special alright. A bottle fed white moose that thinks people are his parents? Yeah, he's some kinda special."

The skies had grayed further as the storm bore down on us. All around was motion as the wind howled. The brook behind Buck's house was tearing the bank away, and with it, the corner of his double wide. I saw the edge of it shift and sag. Alfred kept the gun locked on my face, his hair plastered to his head. I stared at the gun for a long moment. Motion behind Alfred caught my eye. Slowly, I raised my eyes from the gun, following Alfred's arm up to his shoulder, then to the black and white motion I had seen behind him.

Ah shit. Buster the Devil Goat had emerged from the woods and was staring at us with his slit pupiled glare. Or more accurately, he was staring at me with that glare.

Great. Just great.

Buck yelled something unintelligible at Alfred as Buster started to walk around him. Alfred saw him and glanced over with a scowl. Buster regarded him with a steady ferocity.

Sneering, Alfred said, "Get out of here! Get!"

Buster stopped and stared at him. I held my breath.

I realized then I was no longer hearing Sandy or the dogs. Uncle Jim writhed on the ground, swearing.

Glancing at Buster again, oblivious to the peril he was in, Alfred took his left hand and swung it at Buster's head in a roundhouse backhand. "Get away!" He yelled.

His hand clipped Buster's nose. Every hair on his back stood straight up and he let out a "Chuff"

On the ground, Uncle Jim had frozen, staring in open-mouthed disbelief at the scene. Buck was edging toward Marley, his hands clenching and unclenching at his side. I stayed frozen where I was, more out of fear at Buster than Alfred.

Alfred looked back at me, then at Uncle Jim. "What..."

he started to say just as Buster reared up with a loud sneezing snort and rammed toward him.

"Hey! What the...hey!" He swung the gun toward Buster. I sprinted toward Uncle Jim's rifle and Buck raced toward Marley.

Buster clipped his thigh on the first charge, making Alfred grunt in pain. I reached for the rifle just as I heard a loud yell behind me.

Sandy had broken free and was charging down the slope, the flashlight clenched in her fist and with ten dogs at her heels. Distracted, Alfred swung to face her, leaving his side unprotected. Buster was waiting for just that opening. He landed on stiff legs and bounced hard, pogoing up and ramming his horns squarely in Alfred's temple. I saw Alfred's eyes roll up in his head before he slammed to the ground in a boneless, unconscious heap.

I drew a sharp breath in as Buster reared up again, slamming his head squarely in Alfred's midsection for good measure.

"Damn!" I raced toward Uncle Jim, Sandy at my heels. Buster stared at me a moment like he was considering taking me out too, but apparently was satisfied with Alfred. He melted into the woods. "Jim!" Sandy leapt past me, landing on her knees at his side. "Jimmy!"

"Ah'm alright, this is just a scratch, took a chunk out and it stings is all. Are you okay?"

"I'm pissed, but I'm fine, really. What is it with this town and people locking me up all the time?"

Uncle Jim smiled through his pain. "Ah would have to hazard a guess that the common factor in that is you." He looked over at me. "Rachel, are you okay? Why'd you come up here like that? Where's the chief?"

I shook my head, water spattering everywhere. "The

tower must be down. We have no radio, no cellular, nothing."

Uncle Jim swore softly, his voice muffled by Sandy's hair as she hugged him fiercely. "We gotta take this guy in, and Buck, too. Get to the bottom of this back at the station."

Buck. I looked around belatedly, realizing the driveway was empty save for me, Sandy, Uncle Jim and the unconscious Alfred.

Buck and Marley were gone.

Motion caught my eye. A tri-colored hound nosed around the edge of the lot, and two other dogs cowered nearby. More dogs were visible on the hill behind us, racing around and peeing. A flash of white caught my eye: Little Suzy, her blue ribbon bedraggled and muddy, was nervously casting around with a Jack Russell terrier and a Spaniel cross I recognized.

"Hey! That's Luther, Prudence's dog, and Suzy, Mrs. Homas's dog. What the heck was going on up here? All of these dogs were reported as stolen." I called out.

Uncle Jim had gotten to his feet and was cuffing Alfred, whose eyes were slowly opening. A loud crack cut the air as a tree nearby split and fell. We all winced at the sound. Alfred groaned, his eyes fluttering. "Wha' happened?"

Uncle Jim looked at me. "Let's talk about that when we get out of here."

Behind him, Buck's double wide groaned as the water carved away the bank behind it. It began sagging into the river.

"Come on! Let's go. I ain't liking this much." Uncle Jim grabbed Alfred and hauled him to his feet, wincing as he put weight on his injured leg. Sandy grabbed Alfred's other arm and twisted it.

"Ow! Police brutality!" Alfred screeched.

Sandy twisted it again. "Tell it to the press."

With the dogs in tow, we started stumbling back up the hill.

Chapter Forty-Nine

"What about Buck? Where do you think he went?" I was panting as we staggered up the hill, the rain slashing ferociously.

Uncle Jim gave Alfred's arm a fierce tug as he tried to sink down to the ground. His face was grim. "I dunno, but we got other problems here and now."

The dogs rustled and weaved among our legs; already terrified by the storm, they had stuck to us like a pack as we made our way up the hill.

As we crested it, a whumping sound came from behind us. Turning at the top, we had watched in silence as Buck's doublewide toppled into the stream, the walls and roof popping and crashing as the water took its claim on it. Alfred had the audacity to sneer at the sight.

"That dumb bumpkin. He could have made enough money on this place to move somewhere where he had running water, but no...he had to get all sappy on me."

Uncle Jim balanced on his good leg gingerly. His eyes narrowed at that statement. "You really think money can replace someone's home? Their heritage? You really think that? What in tarnation did you want with this, anyway? Buck was babbling about a lab. What lab?"

Alfred tried to draw himself up like he was important. "I'm not saying anything more without my lawyer."

Sandy gave his arm a twist, making him yelp. "Yeah, well, it's too bad for you you screwed around with me. Reporters have resources, you know."

Alfred glared at her. "Oh really, Miss Know-it-all. You think you are capable of understanding business? Hmph." He snorted in derision as Sandy leveled a glare at him.

"Oh, I understand enough, pal. I know who you are, and I know what you were trying to do here. And I know that after burning down Prudence's house and shooting Jim, you, sir, are in for a very bad time here in Brownville."

Uncle Jim looked at Sandy, his hair soaking wet and hanging in his eyes. "We best get outta here before getting into that."

A limb thudded to the ground twenty feet to our right, punctuating his statement. We trudged on.

The cruiser was a welcome sight. A gaggle of dogs swarmed around my legs as I opened the back door. They leapt in, eager to get out of the rain.

"What are we going to do with this one?" Sandy glared at Alfred.

I leaned in the driver's side and tried the radio again. Still static.

Uncle Jim looked at Alfred with a smile playing around the edge of his mouth. "Guess we gotta take him in ourselves.

Alfred squirmed against the handcuffs. "I need medical attention! That fool animal tried to kill me! I demand you call me an ambulance."

"Sorry. No radio and no cell service." Uncle Jim opened

the back door of the cruiser, where ten soaking wet dogs waited. "You'll just hafta ride back here."

He grabbed Alfred by the collar and by the seat of his pants and heaved him in the door. Alfred's yelling was cut off by the slobbering kisses of the Cockapoo I had spied several nights ago.

Uncle Jim leaned on Sandy, favoring his left leg. "Come on, let's go. Rachel, once we get rid of our guest, can you drop me at the hospital? Think this needs to be cleaned up." His color was pale.

"Sure thing." We piled into the car.

Chapter Fifty

The storm had left behind brilliant cloudless blue skies. I slid into the seat across from Sandy at the Brownville Market, gingerly setting my steaming tea down.

"How's Uncle Jim doing today?" I asked, blowing on the hot drink.

"Oh, he'll live. He's still riled up over this Alfred character."

"So what the heck happened?" The storm had created chaos the rest of that day, with the Sawmill reaching historic heights. Between losing radio communication and the non-stop emergencies around town, we had been racing from place to place. Fortunately, the Blackwell dam managed to hold, alleviating the situation. I shuddered to think of how things might have turned out had it not held.

They had patched Uncle Jim up for what had turned out to be a nasty graze across the back of his calf. Alfred had lawyered up and had been taken into custody by the Vermont State Police.

They had found Buck the next morning, unconscious

after having fallen down a slope. He was recovering at the hospital. Once he was awake, he told police the story of what had happened.

Marley was still missing.

We were almost isolated here in Brownville on this brilliant morning. The storm had brought historic rainfall with it, eclipsing the totals from Hurricane Irene. Roads and bridges were washed out, entire hillsides had slipped down across other roadways, burying them under tons of mud and trees.

I vowed I would never sneer at a hurricane up here again.

Sandy was bright eyed on this morning, her giant bag plopped on the table next to her. She rummaged in it, pulling out her notebook.

"Alfred may not have wanted to talk, but he didn't have to. I found out what that weasel was up to, anyway. And Buck filled in the missing pieces."

She started reading off to me what she had discovered.

Alfred Singelais wasn't the successful entrepreneur as he portrayed himself to be. Instead, he was a con man, a flim-flam artist. His record was longer than both of our arms.

Sandy had discovered he had come to town some weeks prior and had latched on to Buck. From what she pieced together, he had convinced Buck to help him with a scheme to get several people in the area to sell him their homes.

The two prizes he really wanted were Buck's and Prudence's land, totaling some 138 acres between them in one contiguous plot. Only Buck didn't realize Alfred had his sights set on Buck's land. He thought he was going to get a fee for helping Alfred buy other people's properties. Buck was broke and had been so for a long time. He was hoping to fix up his house and to make a safe place for Marley to live.

"He told Buck he was going to sell it to some company that does genetic testing, and he was using Buck's moose Marley as a bargaining chip. From what Buck said to a few folks around here, he was going to bring in 'something huge' for the town. He said that he would get enough money that he could retire. He thought Alfred was going to convince the lab that there was something special in the water or soil here. That it would allow them to breed genetically superior animals, like Marley." She shook her head wryly. "He's not wrapped too tightly anymore, is he?"

"Well, he'd been more and more of a recluse for the past decade or so. I guess it's not a surprise. It is kinda sad, though."

"Alfred was going to double cross Buck. There was no lab. What there was is a company Alfred is part of that puts housing developments up. He was going to take those two properties and flip them for a quick dollar."

"So, where did Marley come from?"

Sandy sipped her drink before answering. "Buck found him when he was only a couple of days old. Someone had shot the mother, and she was dead with her calf nearby. She was a piebald moose, according to Buck. Her baby was white, but not albino." She frowned. "What's the difference with that?"

"Albinos have pink eyes. Non-albinos have normally pigmented eyes. I guess he thought Marley was genetically superior or something."

"Huh. Well, he brought it home and started bottle feeding it. And he fed it good, because the thing started growing like crazy. Buck was some kind of proud of Marley. When this clown came along, he realized that and used it to reel Buck in. He was scamming him pretty hard. He had Buck convinced that once the mythical laboratory people saw Marley they would fall all over themselves to set up here."

"I don't understand how the dogs factored into this."

Sandy took a sip of her coffee and eyed her donut hungrily. I waited as she took a large bite. With powdered sugar speckling her lips, she filled me in on the rest.

"Alfred tried to get Buck to sign over his land at first in a shady deal. Buck wanted no part of it, so Alfred began putting pressure on him. He decided he wanted to get Prudence to leave town so he could buy her land cheap. Buck convinced him that if they took dogs from people around town and made them think she was behind it, that would get mad at her and she would be driven out of town. Only it wasn't working fast enough for Alfred."

She paused and took a sip of her coffee. "Alfred got impatient. He had gotten Buck to sign an agreement with him that he would own Buck's property if Buck failed to deliver. Buck didn't realize that's what it meant when he signed it. When he started pressuring Buck to deliver, that was when he threatened Buck with taking his land. He also told him he would take Marley instead. Buck was in a hard place; his home or Marley, which, by all accounts, is his baby. Still he resisted him, trying instead to drive Prudence out with the dogs."

"Only Alfred got impatient and took matters into his own hands, didn't he?" I thought of what I had heard at Buck's place.

"Yup. Buck was horrified. He told Alfred he wanted nothing more to do with it all. Alfred threatened to shoot Marley."

I thought back to my stealth visit to Buck's, from over

the top of the hill, the white fur, the blood. "Had he shot him before?" I told her what I had seen.

"No, Buck did that."

"Buck did it? Why?" I was astonished.

"Alfred kept coming by threatening Marley. Buck had tried to drive him away, but Marley kept returning. The day you were there, Marley showed up first. Buck was frantic to keep him away, so he shot him, fortunately with buckshot, but enough to make him run away. But he wouldn't stay away."

She eyed her donut a moment before giving in. "Ugh, these donuts are so damn good. I should really stop coming here..." she polished off the last bite.

I took a sip of my tea as I thought. "What's going to happen to Buck?"

Sandy shrugged. "Probably nothing. Technically, he could be charged for taking the dogs. But given what duress he was under and the fact they are back home, I doubt anyone will pursue it."

"Not to mention the fact he doesn't have a home now." I remembered the way his home had whumped into the river, taking away everything Buck had owned. I thought of him in a hospital bed, homeless and bereft of Marley. I remembered the scruffy, long red hair of the man who had left a coin so I could buy candy.

"I wish we could do something to help him." I said.

Sandy smiled. "Well, you can. The paper has started a Go Fund Me to help Buck replace his home. Donations are already coming in. What you can do is go see every dog owner and convince them to not press charges."

My phone buzzed. I glanced down at the display. Roger.

I hit decline.

I looked at Sandy. "I can do that. But what about Prudence?"

Sandy glanced at her notes. "Although it was arson, the insurance company agreed to pay when it was determined that it was done maliciously to her, not by her. Looks like she will be able to rebuild. If she wants to, that is."

"Wow. That was quick!"

Sandy smiled. "It's good to have low friends in high places. I made a couple of calls after the fire to grease the skids. She'll be okay."

"Here's to low friends in high places, then."

We raised our cups to each other in a toast.

Epilogue

Six weeks later:

Winter was creeping across the hills in Brownville as Uncle Jim and I bounced our way up the rutted dirt road to Bucks' house. We could hear the rattle of nail guns as the roofers tacked on the shingles on the tiny ranch house that had sprung up. Unlike the old doublewide, this stood some fifty feet higher on the hill, safely away from the once again tranquil brook.

Uncle Jim nosed his pickup truck off the driveway well before we reached the house and stopped. A curious squirrel hung upside down off a pine tree as we opened the tailgate and retrieved a bale of hay and a bucket of grain. I eyed the woods a bit nervously.

"He ain't gonna hurt you no more." Uncle Jim grinned at me.

"Yeah, well, once bitten, or maybe rammed, twice shy."

I cut the string on the bale and began tossing the flakes around.

"There he is." Uncle Jim said.

Buster stood some thirty feet away, his front feet perched on a small boulder. He stared at us with an unblinking stare. At least the hair on his back wasn't standing straight up anymore.

We retreated to the tailgate of the truck and sat as Buster made his way down to the feast we had laid out. We watched him in companionable silence as he nosed the grain, eating in rapid-fire chewing movements.

"Oh, I almost forgot." Uncle Jim shifted and reached into the pocket of his jeans. He pulled out a folded piece of paper and handed it to me. "This came in for you at the station yesterday."

I opened it and found myself looking at a printed email.

To: Rachel Tillison

From: Roger Wentworth

Subject:

I'm sorry

Rachel, can we please talk? I am so sorry. Leaving you was a mistake. I've been calling you for weeks now. I'm back in the states. Courtney and I are done. Can you please call me?

Roger

I stared at the pile of paper as Uncle Jim looked at Buster, studiously not looking at me.

"So, how's Brian?" He asked me.

I smiled. How was Brian indeed? I had gone to dinner with his parents a couple of weeks back, and we had progressed from dating to becoming an item. Brian was doing good, very good indeed.

I crumpled up the email and tossed it into the bed of the

truck.

"He's fine. We are going over to Rangley tomorrow for the Platonic Lemmings concert."

Uncle Jim smiled, a wry twist of his lips. "I swear, you kids and your names..."

"Hey! Look!" I hissed at Uncle Jim, pointing at the motion on the hill behind Buster.

A large white head poked out of the brush above the old goat, worried brown eyes peering down at us. I held my breath as Marley emerged cautiously.

"Holy cow! He ain't been seen since all that went down." Uncle Jim whispered to me.

Buster raised his head and glanced at Marley, then went back to eating. Marley came down and nosed the hay next to him. The two animals started feeding.

"Buck is going to be ecstatic." I whispered back.

"Maybe." Uncle Jim whispered back.

"What do you mean?"

He nodded toward Buster. "Ah think those two done hooked up is what I mean. Means he won't be coming around for Buck anymore."

I watched as the goat and the moose ate in a companionable fashion.

"You know, maybe that's for the best." I said to Uncle Jim. "They're more compatible, anyway."

A gust of wind ruffled my hair. The balled up email from Roger bounced off the back of the truck and rolled over toward Buster. He reached over and snatched it up, chewing rapidly. I stifled a laugh as Roger's apology disappeared down his throat.

Definitely more compatible.

Uncle Jim slid off the tailgate. "Come on, kiddo. We have things to do."

About the Author

Stevie Lynne is the alter ego of Stephanie Funk, a rather twisted individual with an enhanced sense of humor. With the Brownville Series, Stevie allows herself to explore the sometimes hilarious antics and personalities found within small towns all over the country.

Stevie celebrates life in these small towns in a tongue-in-cheek manner while saluting those who make life there worthwhile.

Stevie (aka Stephanie Funk) holds a creative writing degree and has a background in journalism at a small town newspaper. She lives in New England with her veterinarian husband Edward and a variety of furry four legged friends.

You may find out more at https://stephaniefunk.com

Also by Stevie Lynne

Write on Main Street

Sandy Case is on the run and under the gun. When your ex is a vindictive Pulitzer winner with a popular blog that skewers you, the old adage 'you can run but you can't hide' rings true. Landing in a small Vermont town, she picks herself up and attempts to rebuild her life. When a prominent politician is murdered, Sandy ends up on the case and in the story...which isn't the best strategy when you are trying to hide. Sandy has never been one to quit, so she keeps digging, even though she risks running afoul of a deadly gang and revealing to her ex exactly where she is. But will either one of them turn out to be a match for her?

Write on Main Street, the first book in the Brownville Series is available at all major retailers or go to www.stephaniefunk.com for more information on how to order.

See what people are saying about Write on Main Street;

S. Czarnecki 5.0 out of 5 stars A great, fun filled read!

Reviewed in the United States on April 13, 2021

This book was incredible! Fast paced & funny, I read it in a day because I couldn't put it down! It reminded me Janet Evanovich's Stephanie Plum books. Wonderful writing!

By S. L. Funk

A Nickel's Worth of Road Measles

When the past and present collide.

Gerry Donahue is a down and almost out mechanic with a too sharp love of alcohol and a secret: thanks to a traumatic childhood injury he can 'see' past events.

When confronted by a serial killer, this unlikely hero might be the only person able to stop him.

A dark psychological thriller in the lines of the masters of supernatural suspense. See what people are saying;

Eve 5.0 out of 5 stars A dark gutsy thriller

Reviewed in the United States on February 3, 2024

This book pulled me in from the beginning. The main character had me pulling for him, crying for him, horrified for him all at once. I want more from this writer. The book made me uncomfortable in all the right ways that a suspenseful story should. I couldn't put it down and once I got to the end I was completely out of breath. Bring on the next thriller please!

www.ingramcontent.com/pod-product-compliance
Lightning Source LLC
Chambersburg PA
CBHW060713190726
48289CB00002B/666